The Silent Period

ALSO BY FRANCESCA MANFREDI

The Empire of Dirt (2022)

The Silent Period

A NOVEL

Francesca Manfredi

Translated by *Ekin Oklap*

W. W. NORTON & COMPANY
Independent Publishers Since 1923

Originally published in Italy in 2024 as *Il periodo del silenzio*

This book was translated thanks to a grant awarded by the Italian Ministry of Foreign Affairs and International Cooperation.

Copyright © 2024 by Francesca Manfredi
Translation © 2026 by Ekin Oklap

All rights reserved
Printed in the United States of America

For information about permission to reproduce selections from this book, write to Permissions, W. W. Norton & Company, Inc., 500 Fifth Avenue, New York, NY 10110

For information about special discounts for bulk purchases, please contact W. W. Norton Special Sales at specialsales@wwnorton.com or 800-233-4830

Manufacturing by Lakeside Book Company
Book design by Brooke Koven
Production manager: Julia Druskin

ISBN 978-1-324-10609-8

W. W. Norton & Company, Inc.
500 Fifth Avenue, New York, NY 10110
www.wwnorton.com

W. W. Norton & Company Ltd.
15 Carlisle Street, London W1D 3BS

Authorized EU representative: EAS, Mustamäe tee 50, 10621 Tallinn, Estonia

10 9 8 7 6 5 4 3 2 1

PART ONE

C.

If you want to make people pay attention to what you're saying, you don't raise your voice but lower it.

—JULIAN BARNES, *The Sense of an Ending*

Beckett: I speak of an art turning from [the plane of the feasible] in disgust, weary of puny exploits, weary of pretending to be able, of being able, of doing a little better the same old thing, of going a little further along a dreary road.

Duthuit: And preferring what?

Beckett: The expression that there is nothing to express, nothing with which to express, nothing from which to express, no power to express, no desire to express, together with the obligation to express.

—SAMUEL BECKETT, *Three Dialogues*

Reptiles

I ONCE READ—I don't even remember where—a rather stupid statistic on suicides. The research method was not explained, though I suppose it must have focused on failed attempts. Five percent of the people interviewed claimed there had not been any premeditation in their case, nor what might be termed a fit of madness. No major depressive disorder, at least not clinically diagnosed, no panic or anxiety attacks, no to the question on any recent history of traumatic relationship breakdown, no bereavements, no, no, no. Five percent of the respondents—not that small a proportion, when you think about it—admitted that the decision to take their own lives had stemmed from a sudden realization, a momentary epiphany. The gleaming knife that suddenly looks better against your skin than it does on the loaf of bread. The bathtub, and a razor blade resting on its rim. A beam to hang a rope from, and from the rope, your neck. Images that infect the mind with what appears, in the moment, as a promise of purity and perfection.

I have never attempted suicide—I've always lacked the motive, more than the will—but I think I know what those people must have meant.

I DECIDED TO cut off all communication around eleven o'clock one evening in September. It seemed nothing remarkable at the time. Isn't that how everything important starts off?

I was sitting on the sofa between my parents, and *The Siege* was on TV. My mother was the only one watching the film. My father was reading yesterday's newspaper, glancing up every now and then whenever the volume rose with the sound of shooting or explosions. I had just come home from an evening out at the Quadrilatero neighborhood, where I had drunk two oversweet and overpriced cocktails, eaten substandard food, and spent the whole time wishing I were at home instead. I noticed I was staring at the wall next to the television, and thought it was a good time as any to go to bed. My mother was sitting with her eyes fixed on the screen and her torso tilted forward, not touching the back of the sofa; I kissed her on the cheek, then my father too, got up, went to my room. I sat on my bed and started scrolling my Instagram feed. My eyes were burning, the screen was on the lowest brightness setting, and everything looked blurry. I stared at a photograph of a French influencer on the beach; she had a tropical flower tucked behind her ear, and the stigma was like some kind of bait that—if looked at for too long—would suck the spectator into the corolla and imprison them in a hollow, bottomless void.

I opened the home screen and held my finger on the app I had just closed. *Remove "Instagram"? Removing from Home Screen will keep the app in your App Library.* I selected Delete App. *Delete "Instagram"? Deleting this app will also delete its data.* Delete. The icon vanished. I switched my phone off and got into bed. I fell asleep immediately and dreamt I was a reptile.

September

There isn't much to say about me. At least there didn't use to be. There would be now, but it's not something I want to do. Back when it all began, I was twenty-eight and still living with my parents. I had just graduated for the second time, a degree in cultural heritage studies followed by a postgraduate degree in archaeology and ancient history, with a dissertation on Latin epigraphy in North Africa. I was working at my local public library in the neighborhood of Santa Rita. It wasn't a permanent position; I'd gotten it through the state-run voluntary service program I had applied for, and I earned four hundred and fifty euros a month—not enough to live by myself. In my spare time I browsed websites for antiques and vintage items. I hadn't managed to find any kind of employment related to what I had studied, apart from a couple of internships on construction sites. I'd decided to study archaeology because as a child I had been obsessed with Indiana Jones and I wanted to dig for ancient artifacts. All children born between the late seventies and early nineties will inevitably have experienced an obsession with Indiana Jones, but at some point it tends to pass. Yet even when I was eighteen, my dream was still to get lost somewhere in Nicaragua and stumble upon a lost civilization, which is the shared dream of every first-semester archaeology major. By the second semester, you find out that your chances of ending up in Nicaragua or working on research digs are generally fairly slim, and all of a sudden, everything you've been doing seems useless and puerile.

The archaeologists I know mostly work in preventive archaeology. They watch over construction sites and street repairs, sewage systems and cable tunnels, working either as freelancers or on short-term contracts, and always for a pittance. Their presence is necessary because this is Italy and, as everyone knows, as soon as you start digging a road in Italy, some ancient ruin will pop out. This is a small and vertical country, with centuries of rewrites on the same notebook: dig a little and you'll find something you weren't expecting. This so-called cultural heritage is in fact a heap of dead rocks, in such excess that nobody honors them properly, and consequently nobody is able to really cherish them either. What the whole world looks upon in wonder is, to us, something of an old nag, cumbersome, costly, unproductive. That's what the supervisor used to say at the site where I did my compulsory apprenticeship as a university student. He was from Cuneo, in Piedmont, and all his *e*'s were nasal, his *o*'s tight. It was strange to hear him among all the other workers—from Calabria, from Romania, from the Maghreb, their accents so concrete and vigorous. His speech was like something fragile and wilting, a *Mimosa pudica* of phonology, a fossil that would soon be surpassed and covered up, absorbed into the subsoil.

After the apprenticeship it was time for my final oral examination, which I took more or less in secret on one of the hottest days of the year. I went back home to share the news—I'd graduated with full marks but no distinction—and, to save myself from my sister's and my parents' protests, I told them: the university's air-conditioning system doesn't work; you should be thanking me for having spared you the ordeal. It was no use, and my mother asked me if that was really the outfit I'd shown up in. I was wearing black Bermuda shorts, a Lacoste polo shirt, and a pair of canvas Superga shoes. The shoes were clean. I felt perfectly at ease.

Graduation was followed by a whole host of fruitless job applications and some further unpaid internships, except that one time when a foundation with headquarters fifty kilometers from Turin offered me a three-month contract in exchange for expenses and a museum card. I already had one of those. I gave theirs to my sister.

My sister, Elena, is five years older than me. She has a degree in economics and works for a bank: this means a guaranteed salary, sick leave, holidays, end-of-year bonuses, and everything else I'll never have. I have never considered security to be important, but once you begin to understand that the true meaning of "do what you love and you'll never work a day in your life" is that you'll never be able to live off what you're passionate about, that's when you start to feel the absence of something. Though it's not really an absence; it's more like a persistent sensation, an inner voice, an awareness whose origin is difficult to locate—in the pit of the stomach, perhaps, like that lethargic feeling after a meal, or maybe more in the bones or in the epithelial tissue—that keeps telling you again and again that you will never be like other people. Maybe it's just envy for something that's been closed off to you. Every now and then you think about it and ask yourself where you went wrong, if there was a particular moment. If at some point, at a fork in the road, you took the turn less suitable (every time I'm faced with a decision, my mind goes straight to *Pocahontas*, tortuous river versus smooth and steady waters), if in fact you took more than one wrong turn, or if it's just something in your DNA, some recessive gene that's been lying dormant for years until you lost the game of genetic Russian roulette, your defeat condemning you to a lifetime of ineptitude and unhappiness.

Anyway, at least Elena makes my parents happy, even though they try their best not to let on. When we were little, I was sure things would go a different way. She was the one who always fussed over her food, while I was the chubby little girl everyone complimented on her insatiable appetite—the kind of appetite that encouraged every adult, particularly of the female sex, to attempt to placate it. What a wonderful time that was: fed by all into a stupor, postprandial torpor as an existential condition, whole days spent between the high chair and the crib and being congratulated for executing the most ordinary bodily functions. No guilt, no trace of restlessness to accompany the inertia—on the contrary, a sense of pride. Now Elena has a duplex in suburban Turin, a husband who helps her with the household chores every weekend, a three-year-old son who still cries if she strays too far, and, I'm sure, a future baby girl who will soon be on the way. Because people like Elena always have a boy and a girl.

AFTER DELETING THE Instagram app from my phone, I deleted my profile too, then did the same with Facebook, Twitter, LinkedIn, and TikTok. I permanently erased my presence from the social networks I had subscribed to and emptied my phone of all photographs and unused apps. I left any WhatsApp groups I was no longer or not sufficiently involved in, and deleted the chat logs. I did all this in about ten minutes while sitting on the sofa eating paprika-flavored chips. With one hand I picked chips out of the bag, and with the other I deleted profiles. It was a relief to return to the social networks' log-in pages, where they try to persuade you to join them by showing you how to sign up. A simple request for data, as sterile as an operating theater but decked out in garish colors.

Afterward I smoked a cigarette on the balcony and tried to work out how long it would take for Silvia to notice. We used social media to exchange funny videos or alert each other whenever anyone we detested made a fool of themselves on their profile. Silvia had forty-six thousand followers on her account, which she publicly and regularly threatened to delete. This usually happened when she voiced an opinion a little too forcefully and people turned against her. "I could literally say I don't love ice cream and you can bet some ice cream seller somewhere will end up feeling affronted, as if I'd personally insulted him," she told me.

"And he would be right," I replied. "Saying you don't love ice cream is an insult." Then, to console her, I added that if it had been me doing what she did, I would already have been reported to the authorities for violence and defamation. I was much more judgmental than she was. I couldn't stand anyone on social media, not even her. I was appalled by the forms that the cult of the self could assume. Silvia called them delusions of grandeur. "Do you think it's still possible to do things without prefacing them with the formula *A lot of you have been asking me*?" she said. "Who are they talking about, anyway? They sound like they've had some divine encounter or something, like they can talk to saints."

"And do you think anyone's ever quit social media without announcing it first?" I countered.

"Are you referring to me?" she squeaked, feigning offense.

She realized I no longer had Instagram when she tried to send me a video; when she couldn't find my profile, she called me to demand an explanation. It had been a week since I'd last logged on to any social media. "Will you just send it to me on WhatsApp anyway?" I asked her on the phone. That sort of silly content was the only kind I could tolerate—that and political memes. The video in question was of an Irish setter that was tidying up its kennel; the owners had dressed it up in a maid's outfit, with a cap, a white apron, and a feather duster wedged in its paw. I would have bet anything that someone somewhere in the comments was calling the whole thing *Sexist!* or crying *Animal abuse!*, but I couldn't read the comments because I no longer had an account. "You won't last long," Silvia kept teasing me. "But don't worry. When you come back, everything will be exactly as you left it. Maybe even worse."

The more time passed, the less I missed it. It was a relief not to have to read all that mindless, fatuous content, and I felt like I now had an infinite amount of time to devote to other things entirely. The only good thing about social media was that it offered an extremely rapid form of pain relief. It might be constantly reminding you that you weren't worthy, that you would never amount to anything, that you had nothing to show for yourself, but a moment later the anger and the envy would disappear, submerged by the impelling need to buy a pair of shoes or a kitchen blender you didn't even know you wanted. Now I could skip the negatives and concentrate only on my own needs. When I wasn't working, when I was on a break, I would start browsing in search of objects I was never going to buy, information I hadn't been privy to, words in languages I didn't speak, as if I were still fourteen years old and being presented with the Internet for the first time. People's insipid lives, their unsolicited opinions, the criticism of social media posted on social media, the latest controversies, the spitefulness, the unverified information, the performative activism and the greenwashing: all of it now flowing into a narrative you know nothing about, a TV show everyone has an opinion on but that you don't follow. Have you seen the latest episode of . . . ? No, I don't know anything about it. Let's talk about something else, please. "Well done," some people told me. "I once did a social media detox, too. Now I'm back on, but I hardly look at it anymore." And then they changed the subject.

In my purificatory frenzy, I took myself off Tinder, too. I'd logged back on a year and a half ago, a few months after the breakup with Giacomo. It had yielded around a dozen dates, some of which had turned into slightly more enduring connections, though none had lasted more than three weeks. I was always careful not to reach the one-month mark; things always get a little weird after the first month. More than ownership, it was something to do with seeing into yourself. I was scared of the idea of me that I might give others, just as I was scared of anything I could not control. Sometimes I couldn't even control my tongue, particularly when I felt strong emotions like anger, embarrassment, or love. Every time I went out with someone I actually liked, I came home feeling that I'd said too much or not enough and would spend the night mulling over all the inappropriate things I had probably said, feeling too self-conscious to even close my eyes. Strong emotions weren't good for me, so I always tried to end things before I could get too attached. Often I didn't even need some elaborate excuse; when you give so little, you rarely receive much in return. It's a side of me that has always come to my rescue.

The relationship with Giacomo lasted well beyond the limit, and ended painfully. We had been going out for months, both of us thinking, "Let's not get too carried away." Around that same time, some guy stopped me on the street outside the university—he must have been a freshman, or perhaps he was still in high school—and handed me a flyer. I put it away without reading it, but every time I looked in my bag for anything, there it was. It was for an event, a student night, and it said, *And in the end the love you take is equal to the love you make*. I kept coming across it until eventually—I don't even remember when—I succumbed to the temptation of reading it as a sign. I think that's how everything began. Afterward, I stopped believing it. In any case, it doesn't hold true for everyone, not in the same way. Clearly I had been wrong: some people give everything they can and all they get back is a slap in the face, while others are warm and loving and summon love to them. And some are like cats: they curl up in a corner, where others approach them, cuddle them, pick them up and hold them close. The more they try to run away, the more they're chased. I've never understood if it's some innate quality in them, like charisma or talent, or if it's all a strategy. I'm not even sure whether it's a gift or a curse. What happens, in the end, when you get tired of running away?

I'd met Giacomo on Tinder too, back when I had not tormented myself so much and didn't mind meeting new people. In the very early stages of a relationship, I always had full control of everything: I could be whoever I wanted to be, and I felt comfortable. On the app, after a first sweep of photos and bios to rule out those who'd put up motivational quotes, shirtless pictures, or photos at the gym or in the mountains, I tried not to waste too much time texting; if the guy seemed capable of holding a conversation and to possess a modicum of a sense of humor, I made sure to meet him as quickly as possible, to see what impression he'd make in person. I usually considered myself lucky if they got their subjunctives right, avoided inserting more English words into their speech than strictly necessary, and knew how to use a napkin. It was trickier to find someone who would know right away that when I mentioned De Rossi I didn't mean the football player, someone who didn't think Theodor Mommsen must be the front man of some post-grunge band, someone who wouldn't burst out laughing if I started talking to him about the mausoleum of Lucilius Paetus (whose surname sounded like the Italian word for *fart*). I didn't blame any of them, though; if anything, I blamed myself for choosing such a thankless subject to specialize in. Giacomo knew nothing about epigraphy, but he was a film buff. It wasn't something he really told people about, as film was such a banal thing to be interested in. He preferred to share this commonplace passion of his with very few people, if anyone at all. He would spend hours collecting information on this or that director without ever giving anything in return—no forums, no cinema-related social networks, no posts to recommend some rare find or share a particularly beautiful frame. He would memorize useless facts and carefully watch the credits all the way through to the very end; he loved going to the cinema alone, usually in the afternoon, when there was hardly anyone else there except for retirees.

He showed up to our first date wearing a black hoodie with no text or brand logos on it and a pair of dark jeans. He had very short hair and dark circles under his eyes, and the eyes themselves were deep-set and suspicious, like a TV murderer's, where you see them and think, Well, they should have known something was up. I asked him if he'd had a late night or if he was a serial killer. "The latter," he replied. "But only in my free time." He was eight years older than me, and I wondered what I was going to be like at the age of thirty-four. It was the first time I'd ever asked myself anything of the sort, and I told him so. He replied that having that kind of thought is the first sign of aging. Then we sat at our table in the Argentine restaurant he had picked, in the Quadrilatero, and embarked on a fairly unremarkable first-date conversation, during which I cracked jokes about the names of the items on the menu so as to talk as little about myself as possible, and he told me a whole bunch of lies in order to reveal as little of himself as possible.

October

Silvia had been living alone since she'd turned eighteen. Her family was even more conventional than mine and decidedly more bourgeois; they lived up on the hills, and Silvia had always hated being so far from the city. When we were in high school she would often stay at my house, sleeping in the room I shared with Elena, on the trundle bed underneath mine, and my sister couldn't stand her because Silvia always stayed up late and demanded that we talk to her because she was afraid of the dark. I found it funny that a girl as big as she was, nearly six feet tall, and whom I had seen more than once getting into physical fights, could have such a childish phobia. I would tell her about my day or about the first thing that popped into my head and she would fall asleep to the sound of my voice. She had begun to get modeling jobs when she was seventeen, and shortly after graduation she started getting booked for photo shoots and runway shows. She traveled a great deal, but she was often in Milan and had bought a place there, together with a few other girls from her agency—the kind she called "ignorant hotties" because they had grown up worshipping *Gossip Girl* and Victoria's Secret and thought that Phoebe Philo's work at Céline amounted only to the Audreys and the handbags, and now they saw fashion merely as an excuse to make money and put themselves on display.

In the meantime, Silvia had also begun to study fashion design at NABA and only socialized with people from that circle, leading her to develop certain affectations and an aura of superiority that I could barely tolerate, which caused us to stop hanging out. After a few years she grew tired of it and returned to Turin—a city I'd once heard one of her classmates describe as a subsidiary of Milan for poor people and hipsters, where middle-class ladies pretended they were in Paris and teenagers that they were in Berlin—and at that point we started meeting up again. She still got booked every now and then for fashion or lingerie photo shoots—mostly in Italy now, rather than abroad—and occasionally she also worked as a stylist, if only to make ends meet. Silvia's follower count had grown during the lockdown, but her manager still didn't think she had enough. She told her off for not interacting with her followers regularly, for not posting enough, for starting recurring features or Q&As only to abandon them without explanation, for not sharing enough looks, for being too impetuous and brash, for not nurturing her community. "All true," Silvia would remark as she rolled a cigarette, the filter squeezed between her lips making all her vowels sound the same. "Most of my followers are horny forty-year-olds and teenagers incapable of providing for themselves. They don't even know how to google things. And it's absolutely true," she would conclude, lighting her cigarette, "when they say that your community represents you." I felt lucky not to have a community that represented me.

Silvia had bought herself a loft apartment on Lagrange Street, half paid for with the earnings she hadn't yet squandered, half with her parents' money. I loved that apartment, but she had grown to loathe it, partly because of the neighbors, who scowled at her every time she stepped out onto the balcony or the landing looking, in their view, inappropriate—which I suspect was a common occurrence, given Silvia's impatience with the tenets of common sense, particularly when it came to connecting outfits with occasions—and partly because of some unpleasant memories connected to a series of relationships that had begun and ended within those walls. But when she was in a good mood, she would invite me to come round and we would watch *The X Factor*, *MasterChef*, or *Peking Express*, smoke, drink Tennent's, and eat savory snacks and mini pizzas or ice cream straight from the tub. "Thank God for *body positivity*," she would say. Her fridge was always empty, apart from a few beers and a dozen or so bottles of sparkling water, and I suspected—perhaps rather presumptuously—that she waited for me for nourishment. We saw each other once or at most twice a week. If she was feeling melancholy, we would either eat out or pick somewhere in the city center to go for a drink.

Ever since Giacomo and I had broken up, I spent most evenings at home. I watched movies with my parents, making do with what was on TV if we were too lazy to pick something on Netflix. They went to bed at eleven at the latest, at which point I had the house all to myself. I would stay up until one, sometimes two, leaving the TV on with the volume turned really low, and watch a random show or some reality TV until I was too tired to go on, and sometimes I fell asleep on the sofa. Lying in bed, surrounded by the absolute silence of the house—a silence interrupted only by my parents' deep breathing from the other room—I tried to make out if there were any other sounds I could hear. A voice trapped in my eardrum, a trace and imprint of some old memory. I would let my thoughts loose and words would come to me, disconnected, broken, spoken by different and unrecognizable voices, but softly, as if they were trying to lull me to sleep. And so I would fall asleep. But there was no sound coming from inside me.

IN THE LIBRARY, when I had nothing else to do, I observed the people sitting at the tables. Sometimes I made a mental note of their movements and listened for their individual sounds. Libraries are not silent, not in the way people think: there are a myriad of tiny sounds, muted, muffled noises, like the kind you hear underwater. Every now and then, clumsiness and disorder come to the surface: a chair abruptly pushed back, a pen falling to the floor, a book placed down too roughly, a coughing fit. Over the background micro-hum of the polite breathing of a dozen lungs, the gentle turning of pages, the water flowing through radiator pipes, these sudden interjections sound like cannon fire. I watched as people's eyes widened, as they gestured apologetically, then regained their composure. They looked to me like deer that had strayed outside their natural habitat and were now forced to sit still, turning the pages with their hooves.

Unlike other animals, human beings are not capable of adapting to silence: they demonstrate their imperiousness in part through their urge to tame silence, to make it their own in some way. To make it into something less clean, something that will not constantly remind them of how their disproportionately developed intellect makes the way they move seem ridiculous, renders them physically inept and totally incapable of the harmonious, ineffable fluidity that other animals possess. I wondered if social norms were nothing but a reflection of our desperate desire to break with our animal ancestry. On the street, on my way home, I heard the same graceless noises and thought about the silence at the origin of things, the cold and the dark. I pictured endless days, like when you're little and everything is surprising and enormous.

"What do you want?"

Elena was patient and courteous, polite to everyone. With me, a little less so. I always boasted to her that I knew this side of her she tried so hard to hide from the rest of the world.

I usually suggested we meet up whenever I needed advice or sanctuary, but to her it must have seemed I was only using her to vent and curse, usually about our parents. This almost always happened after an argument. Elena was very good at not taking sides, meaning that she never fully agreed with me or with them. There was one thing we concurred on: our parents had many obsessions and peculiarities, and they were only getting worse with age.

But that day I hadn't gone to her to complain.

"I think the time has come to follow your advice," I told her. It was a Saturday; I'd had to take two buses to get to her house and had gotten rained on while I waited for the second bus—which, as usual, had been running late. Elena had been so alarmed to see me knocking on her door at such short notice, having braved rain and public transport, that she'd asked Marco to take Elia outside and give us some time alone.

"What advice?" she said, looking at me with her head tilted to one side like a puppy.

"I think I'm going to look for a place to stay."

"By yourself?"

"Yes."

"Thank God."

"Indeed."

I was the only person she was ever smug with; it was our little secret. When there were other people around, she was the model daughter, while I was surly and arrogant. I considered sarcasm a quality to be tended to, a negative inclination dealt to you by chance but that rather than trying to eradicate, you grew inexplicably fond of and held close, like those white mushrooms that popped up unexpectedly in flowerpots sometimes. I never plucked them out. But Elena saw it as something to be ashamed of, unless she was with me—and this, more than anything else, made me feel gratified. I thought—in fact, I knew—that this was a mode of communication she reserved for me and nobody else, a code we had shared since time immemorial.

"Have you found a job?"

"Possibly. I won a call for applications."

"You won? And this is how you tell me?"

"It's not permanent. Obviously. One-year contract. They want me to digitalize their catalog. It's at the university, though. Philosophy department."

"Sounds great."

"It's a dream. The best part is they pay double what I'm getting now. A whole nine hundred euros a month—imagine that. But at least I'll be able to follow your advice and get out of there."

"Good. Have you already found a place?"

"No. I only started thinking about it last night. And I made the decision this morning. You're the first person I've told."

It seemed this was all she'd been waiting for. She grabbed her laptop, put it on the kitchen table, and started looking through property websites. "Do you want to live alone or share with others?" she asked.

"Do you really think I'd ever go and live with strangers?"

"I guess not," she replied absentmindedly. In the filters, she deselected "single room" and "shared room." Then she asked me how much I was willing to spend. "I'm poor," I said. "I don't need it to be big or beautiful—I just want to get out."

At this point Elena stopped typing. "Did something happen?" she asked, looking at me.

I shook my head.

"No. But you're right, it's about time. I want to be on my own for a little bit. And I think Mum and Dad can't stand me anymore."

"I'm not surprised. In fact, I'm more surprised it took you this long to make your mind up. Still," she said, then paused with the fingers of her right hand still resting on the mouse. "If there was something wrong, you'd tell me, wouldn't you?"

"Everything's fine. In fact, it's better now than it's been for months. It keeps getting better and better."

Elena looked at me for a little longer, then resumed her search. It was almost dark outside, and soon we would no longer be alone. I remembered afternoons at home, just the two of us, when she was old enough to be allowed to pick me up and walk me home from school and make pasta for both of us, and I was not yet present enough to remember any details—only a sense of infinite bliss coming from the winter light that crept over the living room floor, slowly leaving it behind, the TV being on at lunch, the toy commercials, the coldness of the floor tiles across the edge of the carpet. The sense of a dramatic ending brought about by the sound of my mother's footsteps in the stairwell—I knew they were her footsteps; I wouldn't have mistaken them for anyone else's—and finally the key turning in the lock, the sound of a moment in time dissolving to realign with the way it usually flowed.

"Look at this one. Three hundred and fifty square feet, three hundred and eighty euros. One bedroom. So you won't have to cook and sleep in the same room."

I looked at the screen, went through the photographs. I liked the area; you could get to the city center easily and you were close to the river Dora. The listing said it was "available immediately." Fourth floor, large windows. No one would be able to see me.

November

The apartment was furnished with the essentials: secondhand items and cheap, low-quality department store furniture. The paint was flaking off some of it already, and the kitchen cabinets weren't level. It was my mother who spotted that, her expression souring. When she saw that the mattress was stained, she began to make a scene. We had a loud argument, during which I accused her of being an intolerable control freak and she reproached me for being intractable and oversensitive. The truth was that I liked the apartment, which felt like the first sensible thing I had done in a long time, and I didn't want her to ruin it with her expectations. It was my decision, it was all I could afford, and it felt like quite a lot already. Finally my mother decided to buy me a new mattress—she called the landlord herself to demand that he "come here and dispose of this crap"—and I was left, as was the case after every argument, repeating to myself the words we'd flung at each other, the ones I could have added and the ones I should never have spoken, stranded between feeling that I hadn't been understood and the fear that I had crossed a line.

The only thing missing was a television. I bought one on sale before I'd even moved my clothes and bed linens in. I put it in the bedroom: I'd always dreamt of watching movies while lying under the duvet, just as I used to do over at Giacomo's place. Sometimes we would order Chinese food, hoping it would come in those boxes shaped like truncated pyramids that you saw in Woody Allen films. It happened very rarely. But in any case, we would eat in bed while watching a movie. It was always Giacomo who picked the film; I left it to him. Afterward, when it was over, we would talk about it. If, for whatever reason, we hadn't liked what we'd watched, we started talking about it as soon as the credits began to roll. We exchanged our impressions, our theories on why it hadn't quite worked, what had been missing and what was superfluous. Sometimes we played at coming up with the most absurd, most far-fetched explanations we could think of: "The plot would have been more believable if only the heroine's mouth had been smaller" or "It was the couch's fault. That rust-colored couch ruined the whole atmosphere."

In truth, I was mostly the one who did this, whereas Giacomo was always able to analyze the film's weaknesses and put forward valid and surprising alternatives. Sometimes he went along with my game, and sometimes it irritated him. I was good at finding things that didn't quite fit, the continuity errors—a lock of hair that was swept to the right in one frame and to the left in the next, the hem of a shirt suddenly untucked, then tucked in again in the reverse shot. I had little else to offer, so this was the kind of thing I pointed out to him. At first he would nod along, but eventually he started calling it "small fry," all in the same tone with which he would dismiss a film that might get a one- or two-star rating at most. But Giacomo had made me promise that if the movie was good—a four- or five-star film, say—I would not say a word. We would sit in silence and watch the credits through to the end; then we would turn the TV off, hold each other, and just lie there like that, easing into the darkness until we fell asleep. "If there's nothing to add, then why even talk about it? We'd only ruin it," he told me. "But what if I haven't understood it?" I protested. "You'll get it if you try, you'll see. You just need to think about it." I could see it in his eyes when he liked a film; sometimes it was enough to just listen to his breathing, so I would watch him without turning around, sinking into the pillow beside him and trying to make my mind work the same way his did.

THAT WAS HOW I spent my first few days living in the new apartment: lying in bed, ordering takeout on the delivery apps, microwaving canned soup and frozen meals. There was central heating in the building and the Internet hadn't been installed yet, but I'd managed to connect to the Wi-Fi from the restaurant downstairs. It was password protected, but all I had to do was go down there and order takeout, roast beef with potatoes and a bottle of wine, and—while I waited for the food—politely ask for the Wi-Fi password, claiming to have used up all my mobile data. Thirty-seven euros had seemed a perfectly reasonable price to pay for dinner and an ADSL connection that might have been a little slow but was virtually unlimited.

The electricity bills were still issued to the landlord, who would forward the emails to me and have me reimburse him every month with the rent. The landlord was a rather odd middle-aged guy, very thin and always dressed in the same way—dark hiking pants, gray fleece, shapeless waterproof jacket—who did not speak much and was not familiar with irony. I had gone with Silvia to sign the contract. We were a little tipsy from having drunk two predinner cocktails each, and we talked really loudly the whole time. "The listing says the apartment comes with a *generous vestibule*," said Silvia. "Does that mean it's the kind of vestibule that always gives more than it takes?" I laughed, not so much at the joke itself as at the absurdity of the situation, and then I added that perhaps it was a vestibule that didn't know how to set boundaries or how to say no. The owner remained impassive, holding the contract in one hand and a pen in the other, which made me laugh even harder. "I can't believe he didn't just rip it up right then and there," I told Silvia once we'd left. "No way," she replied. "He loves us already. Especially me." Then she lit one cigarette, offered me another, and exclaimed: "You have a home, Martinez! Aren't you glad?"

I told her yes, in the same automatic way you say *Fine* to a throwaway *How are you*. I loathed that kind of question, but Silvia couldn't possibly know that: it was one of the many things I hadn't shared with her. Those kinds of questions made me feel inadequate in a way I struggled to explain even to myself.

In the mornings I went to the library, where I kept furiously checking the time on my phone. I had informed them that I was going to quit to start working on a project at the university, but that job was meant to start in December, so I had decided to work through the rest of the current month. I gave one-word answers to any requests that came my way, as if every syllable required enormous effort to produce. When people asked me for a particular book, I responded with gestures, and when I really had no choice but to give them instructions—which I would ordinarily have whispered anyway, given the enforced silence around us—I got into the habit of writing them down. If anyone looked suspicious or surprised or intrigued, I would put my finger to my lips and offer a faint smile. The only thing

I cared about was getting back home, locking the door behind myself, and curling up under the duvet. I'd heat a pizza up in the oven, add spicy salami and extra mozzarella on top, cut it into quarters, and wolf it down while I watched some action film or mediocre thriller borrowed from the library's audiovisual collection. I had brought my old DVD player from when I was little into the new apartment, and incredibly it still worked. On Sundays I went to my parents' house for lunch, while on Saturdays I ate breakfast late and turned it into lunch. If it was cold out, I'd make some broth with a stock cube and throw in two eggs whisked with Parmesan cheese. It was what my mother used to make me when I had a fever and couldn't go to school. When it comes in contact with the heat, the egg curdles, and it feels like eating monster brains.

In the afternoon, if I felt like it, I would go out for a walk. Elena rarely came to visit, and usually we met up on Sundays. Sometimes she came to pick me up in her car, and before we drove off, she pretended she needed the toilet as an excuse to go upstairs and check that everything was in order. I was convinced this was the least invasive way my mother had found to keep an eye on me. It made me feel like I was still a teenager. "If you find any powder next to the sink, don't get rid of it, it's very expensive!" I would shout after Elena. "Idiot," she replied. "Do you need anything, by the way?"

Silvia and I saw each other more often. Now she came over to my place too, we ate something together, and if we felt like it, we went out. Silvia's friends were weird, used to saying whatever they wanted without thinking about it too much, and some part of me envied them. They were noisy, they picked their outfits carefully, and their chatter always managed to overwhelm the music, so that in the end, everyone inevitably noticed their presence. Sometimes I wondered if spending time with them was actually good for me, because after a week surrounded by the silence of the library and the tinny voices from the TV at home, seeing them was like shock therapy. It took me time, every weekend, to readjust, and there was always some discomfort there, like you feel in your pupils when you move from darkness into bright light or when you suddenly wake up at night with some impelling urge, such as needing to pee, and you have to slip out from under the duvet and walk across the freezing apartment. Sometimes I wished I were a character in a book or a film, the kind who doesn't have friends and seems to have no life, to have never had a life, those characters from indie rom-coms who devote their every waking moment to the soulmate they've just met, with never so much as a friend or a relative calling up to ask where they've disappeared to.

The one person I knew in real life who came closest, in this sense, to fiction, was Giacomo. He had a special affinity with secrecy, as if falsification were his sole credo. When we first met, he told me he worked in the municipal offices and that he had three sisters; he changed his story five times. He was constantly changing it, about any aspect of his life. In his hands, truth was like modeling clay, to be shaped and reshaped at a moment's inspiration. He would hand me his creation, then take it back again without saying anything, tearing it out of my hands, shaping it anew. I'd be stunned, amazed, helpless, waiting to receive this new molding of reality.

I did not have the power to distinguish falsehood from truth; nor was I interested in doing so. It seemed to me that honesty was made of harder matter, that it need not necessarily coincide with truth, and that it could survive all kinds of manipulation unscathed. I remained silent, waiting to discover all the new stories Giacomo was going to make up for me, while he himself looked always the same and always different to me, like a twisted balloon—now a flower, now a dog, now a butterfly. He would tell me he had no friends, then that all his friends were elderly or living in faraway countries. His phone—an old-school Nokia with no Internet connection—rarely rang. He was not on any social networks, and he did not appear when you searched for his name online. I never met his family, so I never found out whether he really did have brothers and sisters, what kind of people his parents were, whether he'd ever had any.

He had been the first to tire of this, near the end of our relationship, and sought to slowly dismantle the barriers he had erected. What had confounded him was my curiosity—not toward the true nature of things, but toward this game he had started. By then I no longer cared who he really was. If everything was a fiction, then I too could be whoever I wanted to be—or, rather, I could be nobody. It was the first time I had ever felt so understood. "That's where I went to high school," he'd told me one day, taking my hand as we walked along the Po. "You've already told me that," I had replied. "You're not allowed to repeat yourself." We had just had an argument—it had been prompted by something trivial, me teasing him because he hadn't replied to one of my messages—and he'd asked me: "Do you worry that I might be seeing other girls, when you don't hear from me for a few days?"

"You're always so transparent with me. Why wouldn't I believe you?" I had replied.

He'd broken up with me the week after that. The company he worked for was about to embark on a project in Venezuela, and he'd been asked to go. "What company?" I asked. He shook his head. "You know I'm no good with long-distance communication. You should find someone who is more similar to you." Those were at least two truths in a row. We had recently watched *Some Like It Hot*, where Tony Curtis breaks up with Marilyn Monroe with roughly the same excuse, but with a diamond bracelet to make up for it. I hadn't burst into tears and I hadn't chased after him, although part of me wanted to cling to his legs like a child on the first day of preschool. But keeping that part of me under control was my speciality. I'd walked away, telling him, "Bon voyage," and that evening I'd deleted his number and all the text messages we'd ever exchanged. Then I'd spent the next month googling his name, adding *Venezuela—Italian companies Caracas—multinationals Latin America—outbound flights* to the search terms.

The guys I dated after him all seemed predictable to me. There was a specific feeling I was missing, a kind of detachment from reality, like a recovering addict who sees the world for the first time without the brilliant, colorful filter of drugs. The people who seemed the most obvious to me were precisely those who tried at all costs not to be. They kept revisiting the same frameworks, using the same expressions, as if in a constant state of déjà vu. I could never tell if it was just me: I had regularly suffered from déjà vus ever since I'd been seven or eight years old.

But when I went out in a large group, and especially with Silvia's friends, I was always dazed to find life passing before my eyes for several minutes, as if it were archival footage, until the feeling finally stopped rumbling between my eardrums. If I tried to speak, I felt as if everyone in the bar had their eyes fixed on me. "What did you say?" someone would ask, pointing at their ear, and from that gesture I would know that I was either speaking too softly or not enunciating properly. I felt as if I were unable to make myself understood. If I made a joke and no one laughed, I spent the next few minutes wondering whether they just hadn't heard me or if I'd actually said something inappropriate. In their expressions, I read embarrassment and pity. I preferred to stay silent, confining myself to laughing at other people's jokes and responding to any questions with the fewest possible words. Three at a time, four at most. Sometimes, on my way home, I counted how many I'd spoken all evening, and it always seemed like too many. In the past I would have worried about the opposite problem.

There was something in me that, in spite of everything, led me to throw myself at people, to embrace and to exonerate them. Never to idealize them—but it was like a state of drunkenness that rose from within some part of my body, probably somewhere low down, and made everything seem more bearable. It was caused by some specter of truth, a rupture in the pretense that made them seem more authentic and granted them fresh dignity. Some kind of unexpected beauty, hidden behind the conspicuous smiles and the layered necklaces, the pencil lines expanding the perimeter of their lips and restricting that of their eyes, because a wide-eyed expression is synonymous with enthusiasm, which is synonymous with naïveté. Then sometimes they'd slip into some unplanned gesture—a childish motion of the hand, like scratching the nose or obsessively tucking a lock of hair behind the ear, or perhaps a look, a clumsy, off-axis footstep, a smile less composed than its predecessors, revealing too much gum and small teeth like baby teeth—and that gesture would, for a brief moment, betray beauty.

Silvia's friends knew all the bars in Turin, knew which ones were more or less popular at any given time, which ones were best for predinner drinks, and where to go when they wanted to stay out late. There were still times when we stayed out all night; we would emerge from some bar with deafeningly loud music to have breakfast together, spilling out toward the river as it began to reflect the dawning day, the city stretching and washing itself, the first few people taking their dogs out for a walk. We ate pizza by the slice, talked in disconnected sentences, our makeup smudged and our hair in disarray. I was cold and dreamt of my bed. I would go home by myself, with music playing in my headphones, listening to Air in memory of a night out many years before, when I was still at university, and a girl from my course and I had ended up at this guy's place, a guy we only knew by sight, and there were loads of people there and we'd ended up drinking and smoking and this guy, who was in a band, had put "Playground Love" on Spotify. I would come home and dive under the duvet, and the warmth and the morning's delicate silence would soon allow me to forget all the ways in which I was sure to have ruined everything.

In the evenings, three times a week, I took a hot bath. I was very grateful to the owners of the apartment for having installed a bathtub. I would do things properly, adding salts and bath pearls to the water. Usually I also put some music on, or got my laptop out and placed it on a bath rack I'd bought from IKEA and watched some classics: Howard Hawks, Ernst Lubitsch, John Huston. When I didn't feel like watching a movie, there were plenty of other things to keep me company. The silence broken by the regular splashing of water against the edges of the tub. If I put my head under, I could hear the sounds of the people who lived downstairs. They watched TV and the early evening quiz shows over dinner, they had two teenaged kids, and every now and then they talked over the program to guess the answers before the contestant did. I would stay like that, feeding on sound waves and floating words, until I ran out of air.

In the mornings my bedroom was cold and tasted of fog. Before I got up and emerged from under the duvet, I watched dog videos. My favorite ones were of dogs in the snow: they would run around like mad and bury their heads in it, biting at it. Their snouts, when they lifted them up, were white, the fur frozen into little spheres of different sizes, and they kept voraciously chewing away at this ice as if it were a hunk of meat. The clips had been shared thousands of times.

What causes people to share things? I would have asked Giacomo, if only I still had his number. He would have said that it was a function of the times we lived in, that people needed confirmation to stay afloat. But I suspected there was more to it. We often argued about what we thought about other people, whether people were weak or lonely. I maintained that ending up having to look after yourself was humanity's most common fear, it caused people to behave in unfathomable ways, and that was why I didn't understand them and ended up feeling lonely. For many people, said Giacomo, solitude is equivalent to disappearing. Was it out of a fear of disappearing that someone had shared a video of their dog? Was it to avoid being lost? Maybe not the people themselves, but certainly their feelings. Feelings are like dreams, transient impulses heading toward the neurons, into the cerebral cortex, and there is no way they can last unless they are rooted out by force, displayed, decoded.

The days were swift, sinking into nights without my even realizing it. On the Internet I read about women who'd become mothers and had suddenly found a purpose, almost as if they had previously been dragging life along with them like an oversized coat that slips and slides every time you move. In the movies they always say that love completes you. It had never happened to me. For years I had felt the urge to keep my hands, my mouth, my eyes occupied. But it was never enough. I was beginning to realize that the only way to stand up to emptiness when you have nothing to fill it with is to keep taking more out.

I HAD ONLY moved some of my stuff: clothes for the season and toiletries, makeup, underwear, and some kitchenware my mother had palmed off on me, second-rate but not so old and damaged yet as to warrant throwing away. But I did insist that all the relics of my childhood should stay at my parents' place. First because I wouldn't have had enough room for them in my tiny one-bedroom apartment. And second because I did not want to contaminate my memories. School diaries and old notebooks, the toys that had survived the passage of time and the books I used to read in middle school and primary school—these were all objects that must remain in the place where I had grown up. Over the years I had bombarded my mother with drawings; that had been my true passion between the ages of two and fifteen, eventually supplanted by an interest in the opposite sex and in the futilities of adolescence. Yet the traces of that time remained in the form of about a dozen ring binders bursting with doodles and colorful drawings. I knew my mother loved me because she'd never had the heart to throw them away.

When I was little, one of the questions that had most frequently tormented me related to the names of things. Who had invented words? Who had decided that water would be called *water*, or that the great gray or turquoise ceiling over our heads would be the *sky* and that our means of observing it would be called *eyes*? In the beginning was the Word, said the Bible. In my little girl's mind, indoctrinated by Sunday school, it had to have been God who was responsible.

I had made a drawing with colored pencils, a bearded man surrounded by a halo of light and with a speech bubble coming out of his mouth. He was saying: "I have decided that the things I have created must have a name; how will you tell them apart otherwise?" In the following vignette, God was visiting a family, hovering over their heads and illuminating them with a kind of light made out of letters, a shower of *c*'s and *r*'s and *a*'s, while mothers and fathers and children sighed, "Yes, at last we may speak!," so that the following drawings were all a succession of "Marco, pass me the salt" and "Of course, Mother, it is on the table"—with the nouns written in capital letters to make them stand out.

In another drawing I'd made up an exercise like the kind I used to see in my schoolbooks. It said: "God is creating words, but he is undecided. Can you help him name things? Underline the words that are real." The drawing showed the usual bearded man with a cloudlike speech bubble coming out of his mouth and a second, larger cloud below, which acted as a throne. The speech bubble alternated genuine words with ones that were made up—like "FOODRING," "CRAWAGGE," "KNOOD." I even dreamt of them occasionally, galloping letters as fast as runaway trains, chasing one other and forming words, some of which were blessed with the privilege of being chosen and ended up spoken by human beings, while others were discarded and soon died out.

It was very stupid, I know, but I really was obsessed. Over and over again I would read the copy of the Bible we had at home, not understanding why the Word did not have a whole chapter devoted to it, but only a single line, with another brief appearance in Babylon, to remove the prospect of peace once and for all. Where was the part on the creation of language?

There was so much talk about bodies, with skeletons and busts modeling human anatomy and science lessons demonstrating that we had descended from primates and before that from water, like fish and trilobites, and before that still from chaos itself, and yet nobody would explain how language had begun. My mother used to say: *It comes from screams, like certain rock formations carved by time.* But to my child's mind, words—these sounds that were anything but primordial, and through which human beings differentiated themselves from animals, informed themselves, and obtained whatever they wanted—must have been invented by some superior entity. Someone extremely wise, a polyglot who, as Prometheus had done with fire, had gifted human beings with words, thus elevating them from their humiliating, subordinate position of two-legged animals. And humans had done with them what they had done with fire: made them into weapons, even before they could be shields.

Every day at work I thought about how the urge to verbalize was always a way to escape one's own solitude, and how solitude itself was still so deeply forbidden, not tolerated, a social stigma that nobody was interested in fighting, a condition that nobody would ever dream of reclaiming and that no activist movement would ever champion. Although Instagram teemed with accounts dedicated to introverts, the people who followed them were the same people who felt the immoderate urge to share with hundreds or thousands of strangers their lives, their movements, their preferences, all that would have once been considered private but now no longer possessed any boundaries, intersecting with the collective and perhaps eventually—due to the excess of content that flowed uncontrolled across the Web—would go back to being personal, and secret, because no one will hear you whisper in the midst of a concert, and the noise of hands clapping at the end of a song sounds the same regardless of who's doing it, no singularity, no distinction, only a fragmented, polyphonic din, compact in its irregularity.

Why was I not like them? I asked myself this question all the time on the way home, with music playing or some podcast so I wouldn't have to hear other voices, and the world moved before me without sound, without a story. In the isolation of my one-bedroom flat, I ate instant noodles and browsed fashion websites—brand aggregators, multi-brand platforms, secondhand shops. I filled my shopping cart with clothes I couldn't afford and then removed them.

The users who sold their clothes on Vestiaire Collective or Vinted had become the equivalent of Facebook friends; I could tell them apart only through their usernames and—on those rare occasions when one was present—their profile pictures, which were tiny and often borrowed from some celebrity style icon or some well-known fashion personality. The clothes these users had worn and were now selling were their line of communication, the means by which their story reached me, only in a more silent, more hermetic way, requiring my full attention in order to comprehend it. On what occasion had Hannah from the Netherlands (*Trusted Seller, Fashion Activist*) worn this long green silk dress by Alaïa? Why was Dominika from Poland (*Expert Seller, 132 followers and 3 following*) selling an unworn Missoni cardigan with the tag still attached? I always chose sellers from the other side of the world, from Australia, New Zealand, Hong Kong, so that when I got to the checkout, the shipping and customs fees would be too high and I would desist.

I rarely completed a purchase; I never wrote to the sellers to request more information. Commerce was the only form of communication I had decided to maintain, the only kind of social activity I still practiced online. Numbers, not letters. Sometimes I would start haggling over a pair of shoes that weren't even in my size, just to see what price I could arrive at. I still peeked at other social media platforms even though I no longer held accounts. Instagram and Pinterest wouldn't let me see more than a handful of previews, so I couldn't look up any fashion influencers for fashion advice—though I had never followed their advice anyway, and had always ended up wearing black jeans or trousers, oversized monochrome sweaters, and leather or down jackets, at most a duffle coat or a shearling I'd bought at Humana for twenty-five euros.

I missed those girls, so beautiful under their ring lights and all the most appropriate filters, their physiques tamed through hours of personalized training programs, wearing stunning items made by extremely expensive brands or medium-budget alternatives, posing in front of the mirror in professionally furnished houses full of design objects and houseplants, and always ready to match fabrics and colors, clothes and shoes, as if it were the easiest thing in the world. Heaven, if it did exist, must possess precisely that level of order and flawlessness. Whenever I felt lost, I looked up a pair of sandals or a skirt on Google and scrolled through the outfits the algorithm presented me with. I filled my shopping basket with related items, then emptied it again. I felt the need to keep myself informed so that I could understand where the world was going, including with regard to trends. I started reading the news a lot more. I had canceled all my subscriptions, including those to the *New York Times* and the *New Yorker*, which I'd acquired when I'd started working in the library, so as to make time go faster and ensure that I didn't indulge excessively in the endless and pointless scroll of social media. Now I was left with the free newspapers. When I wasn't watching films or filling up virtual shopping baskets, I bounced uninterruptedly between one newspaper and the next, between news agencies, magazines, news websites. I was still terrified at the thought that the world could go on without me. I hated myself for this.

December

THE NEW JOB WAS, in fact, a dream. It couldn't have been duller or more repetitive, but it allowed me to not think. More importantly, it granted me the luxury of not having to speak to a soul for nearly eight hours straight, except during lunch breaks, when I had no choice but to utter the odd syllable. I was on probation for three months, after which, all being well, they would keep me on for the remaining nine months of the project. Half of the nine hundred euros I was paid every month went toward rent and bills, but it was so cold outside that I no longer felt like going out, and so I had no other expenses apart from food and the occasional beer with Silvia. I also had some savings. Setting money aside had been a passion of mine since birth—my confirmation, birthday, and graduation gifts still lay in my bank account, untouched—and I tried to accumulate as much as I could by spending as little as possible, with very few exceptions. These exceptions were rewards I occasionally gave myself: mostly holidays, books on ancient art, and shoes, logging them in a notebook where I recorded my income and expenditure. They were both a prize and a break from the feeling of control—a feeling that, I knew, carried the kind of power that might otherwise swallow me whole.

On Christmas Eve I went to my parents' house for dinner, though I would have preferred to stay at home drowning in tubs of ice cream and Christmas films on TV. The plan was to eat everything my parents put on my plate and talk as little as possible, touching only on the pleasures of living alone and how much this decision had improved my life, turning me into a more responsible person; to display my newfound maturity by helping clear the table and load the dishwasher, and maybe even going over in the afternoon to lend a hand in the kitchen; to smile and be affable; to avoid bringing up politics and current affairs, or any topic that might lead to arguments; and, finally, to say goodbye and slink off at midnight, confirming that I would be back for lunch the next day. Then I would cross the mostly deserted streets that led to the city center to meet Silvia and the others for a drink, and maybe stay out until four or five in the morning, as had been our tradition since high school.

That night Silvia was wearing an incredibly expensive turquoise faux-fur coat. The square we had chosen for our drink—we made a point of picking a different bar every year—was crowded, and people kept turning around to look at her. She was smoking slims—the only acceptable alternative to rollies, the only kind that was stylish enough—because it was too cold to take her gloves off and roll a cigarette herself, though her hands were always impeccably manicured and she rarely wore gloves. A guy who had been hanging out with a group of men talking in loud voices stepped away from them and approached us, and he and Silvia exchanged a hug. She began asking him a series of hurried questions, the words overlapping, which he answered before adding questions of his own; he had the kind of voice I would have gladly sought out when beset with insomnia.

I caught myself studying his long, narrow eyes, his feminine eyelashes. Silvia kept calling him Dani: his name must have been Daniele, or Danilo, or Daniel; I hoped it didn't end in a consonant. I realized that I was attracted to him, as teenagers can be sometimes to actors who are not quite famous, and I was hoping he'd just let me keep staring without getting involved. But then he looked at me, and Silvia made sure not to be rude. "Dani, this is Cristina," she said. He shook my hand; he had beautiful hands, too—I needed to stop falling in love with hands.

We got to talking, and he asked me what I did for a living. "No way!" he said when I told him what I'd majored in, and I wasn't sure whether to interpret this as a positive or a negative comment. His name was Daniele. Like Elena, he had studied economics, and now he freelanced for a consultancy firm, though in practice he worked in their offices full-time. He spoke slowly, enunciating every word, and pausing every now and then as if to carefully select each one. I realized I liked people who spoke slowly. They were sure of themselves. They were willing to take the risk of not being listened to.

He offered to buy me a drink and I accepted. We went into the bar together while the others stayed outside to smoke. We kept talking while we waited for our cocktails, and he seemed to really listen to me, though he looked a little blurry—I always struggle to focus on people I find very attractive. It occurred to me that by the end of the night we would probably end up sleeping together. I usually preferred not to wait too long; if I was into a guy, I tended not to waste time and would go over to his place that same night. The hope was that once the objective had been achieved, they wouldn't call again.

Sometimes I did end up liking them more than I ought to, at which point I would tell them distressing personal stories, often ones I'd made up—like that time I told a guy that when I was little, I was molested by a neighbor, or that time I gave the impression I'd once attempted suicide by ingesting exorbitant amounts of alcohol and cortisone. It didn't always work. Afterward I would stop contacting them, but for many, this acted as a stimulant rather than a deterrent. And there were others, too, who became convinced that I had told them those stories as a cry for help, which made them feel chosen somehow, like custodians of a priceless secret. They would bombard me with messages—*Thanks for opening up to me like that. It can't have been easy*—and some would even go so far as to call me up. In those situations, the only solution was to block them. When I told Silvia about this, she said: "After one night together? You're *that* good?"

"Obviously," I replied. "You just have to make them feel rejected."

The difficulty for women, Silvia believed, was that even if they decided to walk around wearing a T-shirt that said, *Don't worry, I just want a fuck*, the best-case scenario was that nobody would believe them.

Daniele seemed the kind of guy I could easily end up telling distressing stories to. Maybe if they were *really* distressing, he would walk away sooner than the others did? He struck me as the kind of person without any problems in life, his path clear of obstacles and filled with love, with parents who still held hands. As we talked, I tried to work out whether his kindness was real or a fairly unoriginal way of getting me to sleep with him. At first glance he seemed confident enough not to feel terrified by a woman who admitted she enjoyed sex, but even so, he might have been too shy or too well-bred to consent to this being voiced openly. He must have a pretty romantic view of love. That, I was willing to bet, was why he had never dated anyone for more than a few months, and never introduced any girl to his parents. Or perhaps he'd only had two relationships, both of which had been lengthy and important. He seemed different from Silvia's other friends. Or maybe he was just better at hiding than they were.

I told him: "You seem made up. How do you know Silvia?"

He asked me whether I meant it as a compliment or an insult. I said that it was supposed to be a compliment, but I was aware that he would not believe me. He said: "Let me decide that.

"In high school I used to go out with a girl in Silvia's class. Greta. Maybe you know her, too."

"No."

"That's probably for the best. We broke up because she cheated on me and I found out through Silvia. Greta stopped talking to us both, but Silvia and I stayed in touch."

So he was a man of fewer but more meaningful relationships. I wondered why Silvia would have done something like that. She never exposed herself too much; she was never decisive. I had a feeling we would probably stay friends for the rest of our lives even if—as had already happened before—we stopped enjoying each other's company or being interested in each other's lives. It seemed to me that Silvia valued quantity over passion, and I found that to be a reassuring trait. Like everyone else, I too was scared of ending up alone and of being abandoned, but my anxiety would cluster around a handful of people at a time, whereas Silvia seemed to feel it indiscriminately around anyone she ever came across. That was why I was so attached to her; her exuberance acted upon me like an antidepressant. Plus, she was a master at tuning in to my silences. They happened every now and then, without my even realizing it, often on the way home at the end of a night out. In those moments I felt understood, a sense of calm and gratitude washing benevolently over me.

Daniele and I finished our drinks and went outside to smoke. The others seemed to be having some kind of discussion, but neither he nor I cared to work out what it was about. I went to stand next to Silvia, who said, "Hey" and briefly rested her head on my shoulder. Daniele returned to his friends, who had meanwhile started talking to Silvia's group, thus forming a broader and noisier circle. We looked at each other a couple of times, both of us pretending we were following the random, uncoordinated conversations taking place around us, and meanwhile some people—the more sober ones—had begun to complain about the cold.

Toward four o'clock, Daniele's friends decided to go home. I was supposed to leave in Silvia's car, but she was still busy talking to people and going back and forth between the bar and the smoking area outside, so Daniele offered me a lift home. He told Silvia too, so that she was aware—he did this in my stead, as if he couldn't wait to share the news—and a visibly drunk Silvia said, "You have my blessing," making the sign of the cross like the pope with his congregation. I stroked the sleeve of her fur coat and, in the hope that she might stop drinking soon, reminded her that it was Christmas tomorrow. "It's Christmas tomorrow!" she exclaimed into the now-empty square. "You have my blessing! Go forth and multiply!" Daniele laughed and gave her the bottle of water he'd bought with his last cocktail. "It's holy water," he said. "Make sure you drink it before you drive—it'll protect you."

We said goodbye to everyone and went to his car. Daniele kept talking and asking me questions as we walked, and I responded in monosyllables, blaming the cold. The truth was that I had begun to feel like a chasm had opened up in the pit of my stomach, as if I'd ingested some corrosive substance. My heart was beating harder than normal, and it felt as if every thump were carving a hole in my chest. I felt as if I could end up digesting my own heart.

Daniele's car was new and clean, just as I would have pictured it if I'd had time to do so. Its smell of car dealership worsened my condition. As we drove, I leaned against the freezing window. I needed the feeling of something strong and sterile to hold me still. Daniele asked if I was all right; I told him yes, I was all right, but I needed to sleep.

I had him drop me off at my parents' house. I kissed him goodbye on the cheek—not the boldest of moves, but evidently even this was too much for my body to handle in its current state, as it resulted in the unmistakable sensation of wetness in my vagina, followed immediately by the feeling of a centrifuge in my stomach. I hurried upstairs and through the dark house into the bathroom, where I tried and failed to vomit. I went to bed, stopping only to take my shoes and trousers off, and waited to fall asleep, thinking of Daniele and of the fact that physical pain was an excellent antidote for infatuation.

I WOKE UP three hours later, convinced that I was going to explode. I rushed to the bathroom and threw up, spraying the wall by the toilet. As soon as I'd recovered a little, I called out for my mother, who was already up and in the kitchen.

"I didn't realize you'd slept here," she said, looking at me as if to register that it really was me. "What happened?"

As I dragged myself back to bed, I told her.

"Were you drinking last night? Did you drink too much?"

I shook my head. My mouth tasted like acid and I thought that if I opened it, I'd end up vomiting again. "Virus" was all I said. "Bowl."

She brought me a bowl, just as she used to do when I was little. Then, just like when I was little, she absolved me from all obligations. "You'll stay here today, in bed. I'll bring you something, maybe some broth. Now try and have a sip of water, see if you can keep it down or if you throw that up, too."

I threw it up. She gave me some medicine, some granules that tasted like mint and that I was supposed to slip under my tongue. "You don't have a temperature. You'll feel better by the evening, I'm sure."

She brought me a book to read. "So long as it doesn't give you a headache. But you should try to sleep."

My throat was on fire and I couldn't talk. My mother sat on the edge of the bed and stroked my hair. "You fell ill and came here to hide out, just like animals do." I loved being sick because it meant I could be ten years old again, and enjoy this tender, nurturing mother who brought me bowls of hot soup and tucked the blankets in.

My tongue felt like it was stuck to the roof of my mouth. I wanted to say something, but my voice came out sounding too low, like a whisper of air. She left the bedroom and I tried to go to sleep. Just before falling asleep, I pictured my mother in the other room and became afraid of needing her for something but not being able to call out to her, afraid of vomiting in my sleep and ending up sharing the same fate as Bon Scott and Jimi Hendrix. I figured I could call out using her first name, Lea, only three letters compared to the five that made up "Mummy."

I had always envied her name, as I envied all short names—my mother's, my sister's, even my nephew's, whereas I had been saddled with eight letters, including an *s* between the first and second syllables, which I remember not knowing how to split up back in primary school, and a vibrating alveolar *r*, a feat of pronunciation that I had learned to master, once I'd turned three years old, by pushing my tongue as far as I could into my upper incisors and producing a sound reminiscent of a drill. My mother would console me by explaining that my name had character, that it had been inspired by Saint Christina, though neither she nor my father had been to church since my First Communion, and by Christine de Pisan, to whom, for a very brief time in her life, my mother had been fleetingly devoted. She would say that long names have character, that it takes time to say them out loud and the extra syllables hold who we are. I did not want to convey character. I wanted a short name; short names are clean and inward-looking. I wanted a name people could let out in a single breath and then leave me alone.

I WOKE UP again in the afternoon and drank some water, the nausea seemingly gone. I could hear my parents' voices from the living room, Elena and Marco's too, and Elia's shouting. They must have finished eating and lingered around the table to talk. Perhaps Elia was playing on the carpet. I kept still, staring at the ceiling and listening to snatches of their conversation. I couldn't really follow what they were saying; the distance muffled their speech and they kept their voices low, and the few words I did manage to make out were useless on their own. I prayed I wouldn't hear my name spoken. I breathed slowly, imagining that I was invisible.

I waited for Elena and her family to leave, and when my mother stuck her head in the room to check on me, I pretended I was asleep. I didn't want to talk in case the nausea came back. It felt like there was something in my throat, as if all that vomit had corroded my vocal cords. But otherwise I was still me, hands, feet, legs. I could move everything. Nothing had changed, neither inside nor outside. My name was Cristina. I was nearly twenty-nine years old and I earned nine hundred euros a month with no prospect of a raise. I had gone off social media more than three months ago and didn't miss it. I saw Silvia every weekend, and she and her friends were the only people I went out with.

Put in these terms, my life seemed really empty. I had lost touch with my girlfriends from high school and university, who had probably all gotten pregnant in the meantime, though without a Facebook account, I would never know. I felt as if I were floating around the room, as if I could see everything from above. The best time of the week was the weekend, when I could get drunk and be less talkative, expressing myself in grunts and little cries without feeling embarrassed about it, and without anyone asking more of me. I hadn't stopped feeling stupid the next day for the stupid things I did, but in truth I had stopped doing stupid things because I had learned how to control myself and to drink just enough to be like everyone else and keep my brain at bay. Keeping my brain at bay was by far the hardest part. I found it easier to do with people, which says a lot.

As I floated around, I became convinced that it all depended on the words that came out of my mouth. People are inclined to share everything, but they don't understand that's where all conflicts, misunderstandings, and regrets begin. Like when you reveal a secret and then wish you hadn't. Confiding in people is the equivalent of masturbation, of binge eating. It is a physiological process that occasionally needs fulfilling, or simply cannot be stopped, and that makes you feel guilty once it is over. I thought of how curious it is that every natural human urge seems to produce a current whose objective is to control it: medicine, aesthetics, the Catholic Church. The Catholic Church made no distinctions: it rejected pretty much everything. But not the sharing of confidences. That's what it was founded on. I wondered if we could still be considered human, and worthy of forgiveness, if we decided to stop talking to one another. If God had made us mute, like salamanders, and if he had not needed to invent words for our use, would we still be his most favored creation?

What was it that compelled us to throw ourselves at other people's mercy? To depend on the opinions, the gaze of others? How could human beings have so little autonomy and be so gregarious? We kept leaving traces of ourselves everywhere, constantly, like animals in heat. Identity did not exist without approval. Acceptance was a crucial parameter, an indispensable form of sustenance.

I considered calling out for my mother, but the urge got stuck in my throat before it could reach my vocal cords. I felt my lungs becoming compressed, and another wave of nausea: the idea of verbalizing a thought or having to respond to a question took my breath away. I had nothing to prove to myself. I did not want for anything. Without my voice, with my tongue resting like a fish that has stopped fighting for its life, I was safe. Where there is silence there can be no misunderstanding, I told myself, no lies or judgment. Everything was easy. I felt like I was suspended in some kind of warm black fluid.

Meanwhile the sun was setting and the sky outside was catching fire. I was lying in bed with my earphones in, listening to "Ça Plane pour Moi" for the twentieth time, off a playlist I'd made back when I still spent time on social media and kept up-to-date on all the indie films Silvia's friends loved so much. I silently laughed every time Plastic Bertrand said, "I am the king of my divan," pretending that everything was fine and that the world was not combusting, as the view from the window seemed to suggest. I had a moment of déjà vu. I remembered that in middle school or thereabouts, they had taught us that in the beginning was not the Word, but Silence, and that if we had been present for the Big Bang, the thing that would have struck us most of all would have been the complete absence of sound, to the extent that if we really had been around in that moment, we would have been able to hear every sound our bodies made, from the blood flowing in our veins to our cells undergoing mitosis to our thoughts overlapping like letters on a deranged keyboard. They told us about anechoic chambers. Like my classmates, I had no idea what an anechoic chamber was, but unlike them, I knew the sound that thoughts and blood made.

I threw my earphones onto the bed, the music still playing. I went to the window and started saying unconnected words, speaking to no one in particular, so that I might forever fix the sound of my own voice in my eardrums.

Still December

THE SILENCE BEGAN, first of all, with an elaborate plan. It's not exactly something you can improvise, just as you wouldn't improvise an escape or an act of destruction. There is always a starting point—a model to reference, a Web search, a book, a song. An impulse that has a certain effect on some people and a different effect on others, especially if the meaning of the message is: Don't do it. Take a group of a thousand people and subject them to as many public service announcements as you want. Even when exposed to identical stimuli, some will react in the opposite way to what was intended. Just like you get with pharmaceuticals.

I once read an article on Pete Doherty. Either the author of the article or Pete Doherty himself—I'm not sure which—claimed that for Doherty, drug addiction had been a slow and pondered path, a carefully constructed plan to become as similar as possible to all the musicians he had always idolized. Instead of concentrating on the music, instead of practicing, he had chosen to focus on the essence. The trouble was that his body—exhibiting the opposite side effects of those he might have hoped for—kept working against him, and did not react as most people's would have. Despite getting high semi-regularly, he couldn't manage to get addicted: it was always his own idea to seek out drugs, never the other way round. So he had gone and procured himself an enormous stash of heroin and crack cocaine, then locked himself inside his house and had not left until he'd achieved his aim: to become entangled in it all, to become a full-blown drug addict.

One thing I knew, from all the literature devoted to and influenced by this subject that I had previously consumed: when you pledge your life to any kind of dependency, be it founded on excess or on privation, like anorexia or doomed love, that dependency will end up taking everything. I was fine with that. I would let the same thing happen to me. I would let silence take everything that belonged to silence, like a kind of retroactive entrance examination for the people in my life.

I WAS OF COURSE aware that adopting a resolute and systematic silence was bound to cause me some problems with wider society, or at least that tiny section of society that I was connected to. How was I going to justify it at work, for example? I would allow myself to turn to writing, when absolutely necessary. A few targeted sentences: *I can't talk anymore. I can continue to come in for work.* Only what was strictly necessary in relation to my tasks. *Yes, no, I need this text.* A series of letters and numbers written on a piece of notepaper measuring three inches on each side. That would be the only concession I made to the world, the only admissible form of communication—not the transmission of a thought, a mood, or an event, but purely that of a position, the location of an object in space, something independent of my will or judgment, subject neither to change nor to alternative interpretations. The point was to avoid sharing what was happening inside me. *Sharing is forbidden*, I might have scrawled across my arms and my chest, if slogans still mattered in this day and age. Though in doing do I would still be sharing something, and thus betraying my own vow. I pictured one part of me, the more inflexible Prussian half, picking up a soapy rag and scrubbing at the skin of the more yielding, performatively rebellious half, and so erasing all traces of writing, like in that scene from *Stargate* where James Spader writes in the sand and the alien girl hurriedly rubs it out because drawing is forbidden.

I was most worried about my parents, though. This was going to hurt them. They were going to ask me why, and other questions I would be unable to answer. Would I manage to stay silent? The truth was that I was weak, as we all are—poor creatures gifted with speech but unable to manage this gift, like a dog unable to control itself when faced with a bowl of food. I would need to wage war against my own nature. I would fight the battle proudly, armed with the intransigence of those too foolish to realize the consequences of their actions, too foolish, at times, to even understand what they actually mean. I would fight it by stifling my voice and my instincts, and, most of all, my feelings; I would be stoic and antisocial, no trace of guilt or empathy, no mercy.

I had reached a crucial juncture in my life, I could feel it, tiny electrostatic shocks jolting through me every time I thought about it, and I felt ready, heart pushing its way out of my chest and freezing, like when you wash with water from a mountain spring. It made me think of the way Giacomo had pushed me to be a better person, the kind of better person who doesn't just settle for things but questions and strives and modifies their position until they find the most appropriate one. *Why are you watching that video on your phone when you could be watching it on the TV screen?*, for example. Or: *All you need to do is buy a longer cable. That way, when you're charging your phone, you don't have to get up every time you hear a notification.* One time he jokingly told me: "Let yourself be conquered by modern comforts," which made me sound like some kind of Spartan warrior.

This was the same guy who'd made me fall in love through normcore fashion and the characteristic frugality of people who are well acquainted with indulgence but won't let themselves be tempted by it. One of the lies I had decided to believe was that Giacomo's parents were very rich, though he preferred not to talk about it—nor could you tell from the way he presented himself to the world, which is often the case with people who are *really* wealthy. Yet he did pay attention to the little things: he knew both the right way to serve salt-baked seabass and the easiest way, and between the two, he never failed to choose the easiest. It was effortless, because all the effort made in the past had paid off. Now I was going to follow his teachings for the first time. I was going to dig myself a nice big lair, putting in the requisite time and sweat, getting dirt under my fingernails, even tearing them off if necessary, but when it was done I would have my sanctuary. And those last forever.

I SPENT THE holiday season at my parents' place, relying on the university being closed and using the virus excuse for as long as I could. When it stopped being believable, I continued to dawdle around the house in my pajamas and a terry-cloth robe, avoiding their disapproving looks. "Are you going to wear that all day?" my parents would ask me. "I'm not better yet," I replied. I knew that they'd already grown accustomed to being by themselves, and my presence there was both a defeat and an unspoken irritation, like a keening from next door that you don't comment on because you know it's coming from the old lady on her deathbed. I didn't mind their looks. I felt good there, and I could not be bothered to go back to my own cold apartment, where I would have to make my own lunch and dinner.

Planning was a full-time job that gave me just enough time to eat two meals a day and make small talk with my parents, to show them there was nothing wrong with me. I had a strong feeling they'd convinced themselves that I was depressed. I'm sure that's what it looked like, from the outside. But meanwhile my brain was constantly on. I thought about how I was going to adapt my life to silence. What I would keep and what would change. Silence was an unborn baby whom I would never hold in my arms and who would never say my name, a fragile being to take care of. I rehearsed the responses I was going to give to people's questions, and looked forward with a feeling of liberation and embarrassment to the moment when I would stop doing even that. I thought about the people who knew me best. I thought about my parents. They were bound to interpret it as some kind of retaliation against them, and that was what I was most eager to avoid.

I SPENT NEW YEAR'S EVE with Silvia, after ignoring her messages for three days. I hadn't seen her since Christmas Eve.

"I thought you were mad at me," she said.

"I wasn't," I replied. "Why would I be?"

"That's what I wondered, too. Don't do that again. I worry."

Silvia never hugged me, not even when she was drunk, while I tended to get sentimental and clingy. But she did occasionally come out with this kind of thing, which would make me want to hold her close; she would return the gesture with a surge of enthusiasm followed immediately by reticence. At this point I would draw back, realizing I was drunk. I felt I had truly very little to offer her—I wasn't a particularly good friend, and most of the time I wasn't good company either—and this was how I tried to compensate. I wondered then whether I would feel the urge to hug her more often, once I stopped talking.

"What if I did it forever? I mean, what if I stopped using my phone altogether?"

"Is this another chapter in your belated rebellion, Martinez?"

She called me Martinez because of Cristina Martinez from Boss Hog. Aside from the name, she maintained that I looked like her, too. She envied me for this. Silvia, on the other hand, looked like Liv Tyler. I envied her for that.

"No. But I mean, is it really so crucial?"

"You tell me. Are you asking me whether it's the right thing to do? If everything really was better in the good old days?"

"I mean the telephone as means of communication. Any kind of telephone, really, even a landline."

"Oh, so we're in prehistory now."

"Right."

"What was your question? Sorry, you've lost me."

"Do you think it's possible to do without? Or are we past the point of no return?"

"Would you be able to do without heating and go back to hunting game and gathering berries rather than popping into the supermarket? I don't know."

"And what about our *friendship*? Would we be able to maintain a relationship the way our grandparents did?"

"Are you all right? What the hell did they put in your cocktail?"

"Answer the question."

"What do you want me to say? We don't live that close to each other. I'm definitely not going to get on a bus every time

I feel the unstoppable urge to gossip about someone. What else am I supposed to do, write you a letter? How exhausting. I hate people who are against technology and progress at all costs. They think they're nonconformists, but actually they're just dull reactionaries."

I nodded. We were in a bar in Santa Giulia, waiting for her friends to arrive. Silvia was wearing a long black coat, a pair of old Céline sneakers, and a chunky woolen sweater. This was how she displayed her disdain for people who spent the year waiting for December 31 so they could cover themselves in sequins: by picking the same kind of outfit she would wear on any other day of the year, which in her case meant choosing among the expensive pieces she received for free from the labels she worked with or the fast fashion and secondhand items she loved to buy and wear only once. We had met up before her friends arrived, which usually meant she had something to tell me. So I asked her what it was. I felt like I was in a hurry, a feeling I was unaccustomed to and that loosened the brakes of my inhibition. Or maybe it was just that I had been drinking on an empty stomach.

"How do you know I have something to tell you?

"Come on."

"You know I hate it when you do this, don't you? It's not fair that you can read people like this without giving anything in return."

"What do you mean, I don't give anything in return?"

"It took you three months to tell me you'd broken up with Giacomo."

"I know. Sorry."

"Three months."

"You're right. Can we go back to what we were talking about?"

"Someday you're going to teach me how you do it. Don't you feel like you're going to explode?"

"Please."

"I really don't understand. Anyway. Davide has returned."

I knew it.

"What?"

"I didn't say anything. Go on."

Davide was her ex—or, rather, some guy she'd had a thing with six months ago. It had never been clear what they were supposed to be. She would talk about him as if she had found the father of her future children; he probably didn't even know her surname. They'd stopped going out the day she had asked him if they could see each other more often and, later on, gone so far as to request that they define the nature of their relationship. What an amateur. This obsessive need to name things was one of many fixations I just didn't get. As far as I was concerned, words were actually the problem.

Now he was back, armed with some random excuse, and they were seeing each other again.

"What's his excuse this time?" I asked.

"They're sending him to Canada for work in a month's time. He wants to say goodbye."

"So he's already given you an end date. How practical."

"Very. There's this sense of a limit, which makes everything even more exciting."

"You're such a romantic."

"Always have been."

Silvia's longest relationship had been with an American girl named Tara; it had lasted nine months. Tara had been studying in Italy at the time. We were twenty-three and she was twenty. We met at an evening social for foreign exchange students under the Erasmus program; Tara approached us and asked if we were sisters, then invited us to share a joint with her outside. I went back in to use the toilet, and when I returned Silvia and Tara had disappeared, leaving me alone and high as a kite. I started talking to a very handsome, very smiley guy from Madrid who had perfectly white teeth, which he displayed at my every joke, acting as if each one were the funniest thing he had ever heard. We spoke in a mixture of Italian and Spanish and English, and I got him to buy me drinks all evening. We made out on the bar's filthy couches, and afterward he asked me if I wanted to go back to his student lodgings, as his roommate happened to be away. I said no because by this point the hashish had won over the alcohol and I felt like I needed to be alone. He was a little disappointed, so we exchanged phone numbers and I promised I would call him.

When I got back home all I could think about was Silvia, as if I'd already realized that something had changed. Over the next few months, and just as I had predicted, Silvia basically disappeared. I heard that Tara had extended her stay in Italy, but after nearly a year spent in a state of semi-isolation, during which neither of them had even been working, they realized they couldn't keep going like that and finally started getting on each other's nerves. At that point Tara returned to the States and Silvia slowly resurfaced; we started meeting up again and doing all the things we used to do, as if those nine months had never existed. Now every relationship Silvia had that went beyond the two-week mark felt to me like a threat, and every time Davide popped up again, I secretly hoped he hadn't changed. Maybe that's what she hoped for, too. After all, it wasn't quite the moment yet for long-term relationships. The phrase *settling down*, one that people around us so frequently used, made me feel as if I were a refrigerator that needed fixing. I was sure that Silvia thought the same, though we never talked about it.

We ordered our second cocktail and Silvia asked me about Daniele. I told her that nothing had happened between us the night he dropped me home because I had been this close to throwing up all over myself, but he'd texted me the next day to ask how I was doing, and so we'd started talking.

"So have you met up again?" she asked.

"Not yet."

"But are you into him?"

"I really am. On Christmas Eve I thought he was the reason I felt sick."

"But instead it was a stomach bug. Nice. Why haven't you met up yet?"

"I don't know. I've had other things on my mind."

"I've noticed," said Silvia, looking affronted, but I knew she was only joking.

The bar had turned the music up and some people started dancing in the area in front of the counter, which was clear of tables. Silvia's friends arrived at ten. There were still two hours left until midnight, and already we were quite tipsy. Alessio, a friend of Silvia's who worked in the fashion department of the Royal Academy of Fine Arts in Antwerp, bought a whole bottle of Gin Mare and had it delivered to our table with tonic water and lemons. He was wearing some beautiful rings, a fluorescent yellow sweatshirt, and Maison Margiela's Tabi shoes. He told us about the guy he'd been seeing, who worked for Dries Van Noten and was in an open relationship. The guy's husband was an artist. Alessio suspected that sooner or later they were going to ask him to move in with them, but he was not interested. They lived in a two-thousand-square-foot loft, but even though the husband's studio was separate from the rest of the house, the whole place stank of turpentine. "That stuff is toxic," he told us. "And the smell seeps into your skin."

Some time ago, Alessio had been going out with an archaeologist who was, among other things, a curator at the MAS in Antwerp. When he had discovered my interest in the subject, he'd told me that this guy also kept his own private, clandestine collection, hidden away in a secret chamber in his house that you could only access by lifting a candle out of a candlestick, like that scene in *Young Frankenstein*. He'd promised me that if they stayed together, he was going to take me to the guy's house so that I could smuggle some artifacts out. I had been very sorry to find out from Silvia that they'd broken up.

We made it to midnight thanks to another bottle of gin. For the toast, we used sparkling white wine, and they paused the music in the bar so we could all do the countdown. The new year had begun. There was that fleeting moment of idyllic suspension when you start wishing total strangers a happy new year, when you love everyone, and it really feels as if something has ended and a different chapter might begin. Then we started clumsily dancing, and I realized how drunk I was when I mistook one song for another and then stopped distinguishing them altogether. The bar was full of people and it was impossible not to bump into someone when you were dancing. Silvia's friends had formed a circle, but each of us kept breaking it and dragging random people in. I was so drunk that I stopped caring about how I was dancing and also stopped watching Silvia's friends to copy their rhythm. We took a break to go and buy more drinks and Silvia suggested we go out for a smoke. It was past three o'clock.

"I'm going over to Davide's soon," she told me. "He texted me, you see."

We smoked right against the wall, trying not to sway too much. It was cold.

"Let's stay until they close, just like we used to. I'm sure we'll all be going home soon. Go on, keep him waiting a little. He owes you."

She agreed with me. We went back inside and started dancing again; the cigarette had got me feeling drunk once more, but now I could recognize the songs. We'd moved on to the nineties. Soon it would all be over. After Cypress Hill they played "Drinking in L.A." and "Porcelina of the Vast Oceans" and then, as the final song, the Faith No More version of "Easy." It was the song that had rounded off all of our adolescent nights out. Silvia and I danced with our arms spread wide, shouting the lyrics. Then the music stopped and we walked out.

"I can't remember the way," she laughed. "I'll get a taxi. What are you going to do?"

I told her I would walk. My apartment was closer than my parents' place. I rifled through my bag to check that I had the keys with me.

"You're fine, everything's fine, right?" she slurred.

I assured her that yes, everything was fine. Then I hugged her and asked her whether she was going to miss my voice. If she would feel its absence, once I stopped using it. Silvia only said "Good night, Ariel," before kissing me on the forehead like you do with nieces and nephews, throwing her cigarette away, and running to the taxi stand on the opposite side of the square. She yelled that she loved me, and even in all that chaos, I heard her, and thought that she wasn't going to remember that either.

I finished my cigarette, sticking close to the wall, and started walking toward my house. The street was littered with broken glass, discarded bottles, and plastic cups, while a few stray fireworks still rumbled in the sky—or maybe they were just firecrackers some kid had set off. I got home and fell into bed without taking my makeup off. The apartment had already begun to feel stuffy; my worn clothes piled up on the chair looked like corpses in the darkness.

It was the first day of the new year. While there were still people out on the streets, in homes that weren't theirs, or in bars, I started thinking about Giacomo, and gave myself another two weeks before I made my decision.

January

TWO DAYS LATER I met up with Daniele. He'd written to me on New Year's Eve and I had replied the morning after, claiming not to have seen his message. I asked him to come round the next day, and so we started meeting up a couple of evenings a week. I told him I didn't feel like going out, so we would stay at home and order takeout. I liked the way he started making conversation as soon as he arrived. He would always ask me questions, and he didn't make it seem like it was all just a long lead-up to sex. He cared deeply about his family and mentioned them frequently. I was sure they must have given him a strict but ultimately loving upbringing, with a sense of Catholic morality that justified obligations and limitations with the search for love, charity, and respect for one's fellow man. Casual sex must therefore contain a modicum of feeling—that way it wouldn't be sinful.

Daniele was one of those quiet, gentle types who have lots of female friends even though they're straight; funny without ever being vulgar; prone, when drunk, to revealing an unusual distaste for hierarchy and the rules that govern public order, and reluctant, therefore, to ever drink too much; discreet but interested in having conversations, preferably with a small group of people; occasionally boring; and with an incurable predilection for manipulative women. The kind of guy I could eventually have lost my head over, if I didn't have anything else to do. I kept thinking about silence, and realized that once I got started, I might struggle, and feel lonelier. It was possible that I might need him.

Halfway through January, I confessed my plan to him while he treated himself to a cigarette after sex. It took him a moment to work out whether or not I was joking, and once it was clear I wasn't, he tried to change my mind. I explained that it was too late, that this was not what I was asking of him.

"But why, though? Maybe you should talk to someone about this."

"It's not a cry for help, and I'm not going to commit suicide. In fact, it's very likely I won't make it past the first week. But let's say I do: then I'll need some company, every now and then. Stay in, have sex, watch movies: all the things we've been doing for the past few days now, without any obligations, and whenever we both feel like it. Just the same as now, minus the talking part."

"I'm not sure I understand."

"I'm only asking that we keep doing what we've already been doing, but warning you that there will be more silence, next time. You can still talk, of course. But don't expect me to react."

"What kind of game is this?"

"Please don't ask me that. I don't want to explain."

"How many questions am I allowed?"

"None."

"OK. Who else have you told?"

"Just you. You're the only one carrying this weight."

"Why?"

"Why what?"

"I mean, why me?"

"You mean among my abundance of lovers? You're the one with whom silences are the least embarrassing."

There was only Silvia left to tell. With my parents and Elena, I planned to write letters. I couldn't bring myself to face them. It's not the kind of thing you tell your parents until it's done: a bit like deciding to have a baby. Conception is never part of the conversation. I kept trying to find comparable examples with which to exonerate myself, since there was no prior literature to reference. But with Silvia, I felt I ought to tell her face-to-face. So I invited her to come round to my place, as I was convinced she would make a scene and I didn't want anyone to hear us.

In the end, she was pretty calm throughout. She politely pointed out that what I was about to do made no sense at all.

"But I'm assuming you know that already," she added.

"Yes. But I really don't feel I'm doing it for anyone else. I don't know—it feels like a vocation."

"Like a vow, then. You're taking a vow of silence. What are you asking for in return?"

"The redemption of mankind. I told you, it's not a vow. The point is, I don't have anything to ask for in return. Maybe some kind of purification. But personal, just for me. Think of it as a detox from words."

"Like when you decided to stop drinking."

"Now, that was a vow."

"Yes, and what for?"

"Never mind."

"OK. This really is the dumbest thing I've ever heard of. And not for the reasons you think."

"Not for the reasons I think? Meaning?"

"Not just for those, at least. You said the aim was to stop communicating, right?"

"To stop sharing. I want to find out what it feels like."

"Sure, whatever. The point is, you're going about it the wrong way, Martinez. Silence is an act of communication. By not communicating, you're communicating something."

"I'm communicating my decision not to communicate."

"Either way, you're doing it. It's a paradox."

I thought about it.

"You're right," I said eventually. "Let's put it this way, then: it's an experiment. I want to see how long it lasts. How long it takes for a human being to stop being different from an animal."

"Animals communicate. Dogs bark, mice squeak, stags trumpet, et cetera. Or maybe that's elephants."

"What about lizards? And rabbits?"

"Rabbits squeal when they're about to die."

"I know, it's awful. But what about all the rest of the time?"

"They might not make any noises, but they must have some kind of silent language."

"A necessary language. Something they only turn to in extreme situations, to warn of danger. Not to talk about futile things. Not to merely express a thought."

"What's wrong with expressing a thought? There'd be no philosophy otherwise. There'd be no art, no cinema, no fashion."

"There's nothing wrong with it. I admire necessary and essential language. Technical language *is* essential language. Just like artistic language. But I have nothing essential to say. Ergo, I have decided to keep quiet."

"What about nonverbal communication?"

"I'm not interested in that. You mean body language, right? The fact that you might scratch your nose when you're telling a lie? It's completely unintentional. I'll control what I'm aware of—I have no power over the rest. I've got limits, too."

"You'll still be communicating, though."

"But I won't be sharing."

"You'll be sharing an inner state."

"It doesn't matter. It's deceptive. All nonverbal language is deceptive. It's not direct, it's not precise, it's not always intentional. All the power is in the eye of the beholder. Have you heard of erotomania?"

"Of course. I have to live with it every day."

"If a person looking at me should end up focusing their attention on the way I blink, or my gait, or where my gaze lies, and see some kind of message in that, they would be no different from the kind of person who is convinced that their favorite pop star is sending them declarations of love through their songs. The truth is that there will be nothing inside me. I will practice silence. Including the inner kind."

"It's a real shame," said Silvia. "More than anything else, I'll miss hearing your opinion on things. Especially when you express them in the form of protest."

"Do I look cute when I'm angry?"

"Very funny. You're like one of those crazy old ladies that everyone ends up being neighbors with, someday."

"Like the cat lady from *The Simpsons*?"

"A little bit, yeah."

"But you'll love me anyway?"

"I'll love you anyway. But I'll never tell you because you won't tell me."

Afterward we went out and got drunk on vodka. It was our favorite kind of drunk to be, because it made us effusive and loquacious. We made friends in the women's restroom like we used to do on Saturday nights in high school and university, and we wedged ourselves into the bar's seating area until the staff came over and begged us to leave, since they were about to close. We talked loudly all night without ever mentioning my plan again.

Dear Elena,

I've started this letter in the most predictable way because I need something predictable to hang on to. Isn't that what conventions are for? Reassurance? But I digress. The fact is that I haven't spoken for a week and I'm hungry. I let myself make an exception just once, on the phone with Mum. And now with this letter, too, though it's not really the same as talking, and now that I've started writing it, I'm not sure if it's you I'm doing it for or myself. Probably for myself, because I need to explain what's happening so that you can all help me with this choice. I'm not just asking you to respect it, as with those somewhat radical, uncompromising stances that people's kids take sometimes. I'm asking you to help me maintain it. Which may be an even more selfish request. But I see no other way.

I have decided to make do without words, at least in oral form. I have decided to practice silence as practiced by people who cloister themselves, excluding the cloistering part. Seven days a week, with no room for respite. It's not a definitive termination, more like a break. A pause in communications.

I made this decision by myself, without talking to you guys about it. When you put it that way, it's kind of funny—not talking about not talking. I suppose you're all more or less used to my tight-lipped ways. But this is more than that, and I know that if I had warned you in advance, you would have tried everything to convince me to change my mind. You would have taken me to see a psychologist, thinking I must be depressed. Or just plain crazy. I expect you'll think me crazy, and maybe I am. It's always spooked me to think that crazy people don't even realize they're crazy, and going crazy has always been one of my great fears. Maybe that's another reason I've decided to do what I'm doing. Because confirming and diagnosing a state of madness passes, first and foremost, through words.

I wrote above that this is a break I have decided to take. I don't yet know how long for: I don't think it's something that should be established in advance. Perhaps I'll feel the urge to speak again when I have something to say. For the moment, I feel like I definitely don't: therefore, as Thumper might say, it's best I say nothing at all.

As for why I'm doing this: in truth, there are many reasons; I wouldn't want you to think this is one of my usual impulsive resolutions. I spent weeks formulating a plan, trying to figure out, first of all, if I could actually do this, but also if there was a way I could do it without causing you all pain. I did not find a solution. But I am confident I can persuade you—persuade you that this is not meant as a remonstration, nor as retaliation. I'm well past adolescence, I have nothing to reproach Mum and Dad for. I'd like you to tell them that. It's not their fault and, most importantly, this is not happening because of any kind of pain. You could say it's partly a rejection, but it's a rejection of what is outside. You guys are not like the outside world. That's another reason I'm doing this. As an unusual act of purification, gifting you the chance to deal with a better person. Giving myself the chance to be happy. I have realized that happiness, for me, must now come through silence. I need to step away from words so that they may recover their meaning. Because I don't know what that is anymore—that's the whole point. So think of me as an early-phase Siddhartha, and don't torment me: it is necessary to go through this phase in order to find the middle way. Think of me as an atheist nun taking a vow of silence to no divinity at all, but perhaps only to human beings, perhaps only to you guys.

I know it's difficult to comprehend. I'm not necessarily asking you to. And I will not feel superior to you if you do not—if anything, it'll be the opposite, you have can count on that (how funny: I was about to write "you have my word." You'll have my silence, let's put it that way). All I ask is that you admit this new Cristina: a quiet Cristina (even more so than usual) who will not be involved in conversations, who will appear—if I succeed in my quest—like a plaster cast of herself, though inside she will be the same. Well, maybe not exactly the same: a version in a state of transformation. Yes, think of me as a chrysalis (but of a butterfly, because those look like green and sinuous sarcophagi; not like the ones other insects get, those are really gross). I will be with you in any way that does not involve words, at least not mine. I will listen to yours. They will be good for me. I will be an impassioned spectator.

That will be enough to help me, I think. It's all I ask of you. I need it so that I can be a better person.

Yours, all of you,
C.

February

THE HARDEST THING, when you're not allowed to talk, is to stop yourself from answering questions. There lies the true endurance test: against a physical impulse that starts from the brain and flows through the nerves until you feel it in your muscles—in your tongue, your jaw—where it rows against every resolution and every imposition. You might characterize it as a response to an external stimulus, as with pain, but that wouldn't be totally accurate; its origins are actually more hidden. I think they lie in upbringing. That framework of gestures and reactions that is our childhood inheritance, laboriously bequeathed to us by our parents, teaching us how to be in the world while simultaneously showing us that being in the world means, above all, forcing yourself to do things you don't want to do. *What do you say? Please. Thank you. Cat got your tongue? No. Where have you been? Have you eaten?* Good kids are those who know how to respond in the correct manner. You learn by getting it wrong, and at some point, when you are no longer able to avoid answering questions, you become an adult. Adults pride themselves on their good manners, on courtesy—which is not the same as kindness—because these are some of the many traits that distinguish humans from animals. And if the evolution of the species resides—or, I don't know, originates—in the ability to communicate, then humanity has surely found endless excuses to make use of the skill.

This was the kind of thing I thought about, in those long periods I was now spending alone with myself, which were only destined to grow longer. One of the first things I had discovered was that practicing silence meant forgetting what you've been taught; and you're fighting against a whole load of muscle memory, a whole load of impulses, and a whole load—years' worth—of precepts. It was exhausting, but I was convinced that—as with any kind of training—I just needed to be patient.

In exchange, I had reclaimed time. The days seemed longer. Without words, I could feel the hours go by, and the minutes, and everything seemed bigger. I recalled reading somewhere that love defeats death because it gives new meaning to the passage of time, stops it, or at least slows it down. Like Zen in the art of tea, or those people who become fixated on rediscovering what life truly tastes like, and so avoid salt and all additives, cook everything from scratch, and only buy organic food, convinced that in doing so they are keeping death at bay. Human beings are so strange, I reflected: they spend their whole lives looking for schemes for passing the time and trying to evade boredom, until eventually they realize that life has gone by too fast, so off they go in search of ways to slow down. It seemed that silence worked just like green tea and love.

The day before the start of the silence, I had gone to my parents' house for dinner. Elia had screamed like a madman throughout, and I had wondered if I was going to miss any of this. The small talk at the dinner table, recounting our respective weeks, commenting on the news. Family dinners were the only kind where I did not have a problem voicing my opinions. Where I did not feel as if everything I couldn't speak of weighed much more heavily than the words I was pushing out of my mouth. I had slipped the letter into Elena's bag before she'd left.

I wrote another, much shorter letter to my manager, Patrizia, to warn her and to explain. I didn't actually give her a full explanation. I lied. I told her I'd been diagnosed with some kind of laryngeal dysfunction. A tumor, I added. A benign one, I specified in a rush of remorse and superstition. I had been advised that my vocal cords needed total rest, and that was that. She believed me; who wouldn't have? The word *tumor* is so brutal that it needs no further clarification. It's like a linguistic dam: use that word, the T-word, and the flow of questions will be stemmed. Did I feel like a total bitch? I did, but such was the price to pay.

At work I was managing fairly well, or so it seemed to me. The trickiest moments occurred whenever anyone came to me with a request, even though Patrizia had warned them I couldn't speak. I began to use Post-it notes to communicate that which I couldn't voice and which was strictly necessary. Luckily, I spent most of my time interacting with computers. I had never got on particularly well with technology, but the computers in the faculty library were reassuring entities. They weren't even connected to the Internet, only to the university network. Sometimes I responded to people directly on the internal chat, hoping they would get the hint and contact me that way. My youngest colleague, a girl who was around twenty-five years old and who'd been looking at me as if I were a psychopath ever since the day I'd arrived, was perfectly happy to keep her distance. She only ever wrote to me when our managers expressly required it, grumbling about the antebellum keyboard she'd been saddled with, the letters half rubbed off, the keys getting stuck at least once a day.

The equipment we had at our disposal reminded me of my DVD player, which both Silvia and Daniele teased me about. "Why don't you use my Netflix account?" Daniele had once suggested. *You're crazy*, I would have told him. I had only recently logged out of the account I used to share with Giacomo. I had turned off the automatic login on all my devices, and thankfully I couldn't remember any of the passwords. One of the most burdensome addictions I had acquired after the end of our relationship was to restlessly check his viewing history. I never knew whether he noticed or not, whether he remembered I still had him logged in. At times I thought he did, and then I would convince myself that the films and TV shows he was watching must be messages directed at me. Giacomo rarely used Netflix, because he considered its catalog to be subpar, and he preferred Mubi, though I didn't have his password for that. But every now and then even he would fall into the trap of blockbusters and lowbrow entertainment or embark on a rewatch of a cult classic he'd seen at the cinema when it was first released. I imagined he must pick these on purpose, watching them on his own, in the evening, and it seemed to me they communicated a mood—pain, melancholy, tepid euphoria. Sometimes I would come across more unusual choices, too—documentaries on the international drug trade, on addiction, on animals and their amazing feats, or Indian and northern European shows he'd watch for ten minutes before giving up—and I came to believe that they were coded messages for me, to tell me he missed me or that he hated me. And sometimes I thought he must be picking them with some other girl, and so I would watch the same thing in the middle of the night, smoking cigarette after cigarette, eating gummy bears or licorice sticks, and masturbating. I often asked myself if he would be proud of me, and ever since I had started with the silence, I had managed to tell myself yes. Thinking about him hurt less. It was an invisible thread that joined us.

As I was saying, I had started using Post-it notes at work. When someone asked me something, I wrote the answer down on a piece of paper. I used the odd stylistic flourish to try to embellish my otherwise sparse responses—a smiley face, an arrow accompanying the text, a bolded exclamation mark with a circle instead of a dot. Sometimes I dotted my *i*'s with hearts. My handwriting became florid. If they asked any follow-up questions, I used another Post-it. I was trying to avoid gestures too, so even the yeses and the nos went on Post-its. I did not keep any pre-prepared ones, though it would have been easier that way; I used fresh notepaper every time.

I was determined to avoid gestures because I needed to limit how far I was willing to compromise on silence, and those hearts and embellishments seemed so far removed from the person I was that they did not feel like a betrayal. If, on my way home, someone on the street asked me for directions, I pretended not to hear them. It didn't happen very often, anyway. It was mostly older people at the bus stop or at the supermarket, disguising their need for conversation with lazy requests for assistance, rhetorical questions, queries they already knew the answers to. I always kept my headphones on, so that often I genuinely couldn't hear them and it was therefore easier to ignore them. Every now and then, when I walked on with my head down despite the question I'd been asked, I could hear them over the music, calling insults after me. Sometimes I would burst out laughing. Other times I felt ashamed. Almost always, I couldn't help but think of how quickly we develop an idea of the people we come across, and how off-target we usually are. This was not something I could control, but I was fine with that. In any case, I was protected now. I had gotten better at tolerating the world.

When I got home, I would prepare some food. I still ordered from the apps, but only when the need to make a sound became unbearable. It was the only luxury I indulged in. That *Yes?* on the intercom, signaling my presence at the other end of the line, was the weekly transgression I allowed myself. If I managed not to utter a word all week, if I was able, even on those Fridays or Saturdays when I happened to go out with Silvia, to remain faithful to the silence, then on Sunday I could treat myself to those three letters, followed by the clicking of the front gate to announce that I was coming downstairs to collect the delivery, and finally a quick *Thanks*, a minor concession to social norms and politeness. I didn't want to be mean to the people who delivered my food. They didn't deserve it, especially not on a rainy day. I wished the companies would hurry up and automate it all; with machines and computers, you don't have to talk at all, and then my life would be perfect.

But mostly I cooked my own food. I had the TV tuned to cooking channels and I forced myself to record any recipes I could easily replicate, jotting them down in a notebook. The next day I would go to the supermarket and buy the ingredients. I always picked the same supermarket, a discount store frequented by penniless students and middle-aged people with inadequate pensions or salaries. More rarely someone who happened to be passing by would quickly pop in before leaving just as fast, mildly horrified by what they had seen.

The discount store had become my favorite shop for two reasons. The first and least important was the variety of exotic produce it stocked. It meant that whenever I was feeling experimental, I could try my hand at ethnic cuisine. The second reason was the cashiers. Spending time in that place, under fluorescent lights and in the humidity caused by the fact that the heating was always turned too low and only left on for a couple of hours a day, made them all disillusioned and not very talkative. The older cashiers, stuffed into uniforms pulled all the way up to their chins, had dull eyes and gray roots showing in their hair. Their colleagues who were under the age of forty moved faster, but they had puffy eyes and empty gazes that always looked the wrong way, like shopkeepers discreetly do when a customer is entering their PIN. No one asked any questions, no one was interested in starting a conversation, and the music, which was always too loud, seemed chosen specifically to remind you of that fact. There were no points or coupons to collect, no loyalty cards. People came in, did whatever they had to do, and went back to their lives. It was a perfect refuge.

I tried to furnish my silence with refuges: the discount store, my apartment, my headphones. People seemed increasingly distant from me, but at least now there was a valid motive. A scapegoat for my inferiority complex. Now I knew that if nobody sought me out anymore, there was a reason, and if they looked at me strangely, it was because of the silence. When they realized that I couldn't talk, they behaved differently. I had begun to notice that even the most sensitive people did not know how to get past it. I found myself dealing with *excessive politeness*, and learned that it could cause just as much distress as discrimination did, that it *was*, in fact, a form of discrimination—but rather than upset me, this thought would come back to me at night and lull me to sleep. Most importantly, I didn't have to think about what to say anymore. I didn't have to listen. My mind had freed itself of an oppressive burden, and all I needed now in order to exist in the world were one heart, two lungs, and all the rest of the apparatus that enabled those organs to function. The tongue's only job was to taste things. The brain could be put on pause. Whenever I felt like I was being watched, whenever I silently wondered what I was doing, why I was spending time among people if I didn't wish to communicate with them, I concentrated on my organs and my skin, on my heart and lungs, and I thought: I have just as much a right to exist as you do.

But, of course, there was the fact that my social interactions had diminished even further. Silvia came to see me only rarely, and although she had no trouble talking for the whole duration of her visits, it was clear that she did not feel comfortable. It was as if she had suddenly become shy. I could sense that she was struggling from how she would pause for too long between one word and the next, as if to gauge its weight and choose appropriately, and from a very light and totally new stutter that had crept into her speech. She had always been the chattier one of the two of us, but now, in the absence of any reaction, it was as if she had become self-conscious, the way people can be the first time they're put in front of a TV camera. But unlike an actual TV camera, I gave her nothing back, nothing to boast about. The best-case scenario was that she would leave my place with an image of herself that was far from comforting, as if I'd functioned as a funhouse mirror rather than a camera lens. When you see yourself reflected in one of those things, the sight sticks in your mind, polluting the image of yourself that you have so laboriously cultivated. I didn't think Silvia would ever get used to the feeling.

"You're crazy," she told me one time. "I still can't believe you're doing this shit. Listen, everyone's been wondering: Is it something you read somewhere? Have you joined a cult? Fallen into some kind of hate spiral? Are you hoping your choice will save the world? How do you not just burst out laughing? It's like the quiet game. If I make faces at you, will you stop?"

She talked really fast and then started giggling. I also laughed. Not because I was amused, but because I wanted her to know that she had missed the point. It bothered me, actually. She was wearing a fur coat I'd never seen before, and I wished she would talk to me about that instead. It was either mink or marmot, a relic from the eighties, the kind you find at the market in Porta Palazzo. The cut was dated and the fur was bristly. I didn't think it suited her as well as all her other clothes did, and had I been with her when she'd bought it, I wouldn't have let her. I tore a sheet out of the notebook I kept on the table and wrote: *Tell me something.*

"You're so melodramatic," she said, laughing again. "It's like you're about to die. Shall we go out?"

It seemed like a good idea. It was almost evening, I had no food left at home, and I felt like having a drink. Silvia was walking very fast, and I followed her like I would do sometimes when my mother was angry with me and I was afraid that if I lost sight of her, she wouldn't come looking for me but would just leave me to my own devices.

"I'm hungry," said Silvia. "And I feel like having a drink."

We walked into one of our usual aperitif spots on Via Po. The owners and the bar staff all knew us. Silvia greeted them and stopped for a very loud chat. The bar was full and there was a deafening din, so her voice made little difference. I smiled and nodded before heading for the only free table I could see. I sat and waited for her, reading the news on my phone and browsing the notifications from Vinted and Vestiaire, which informed me that the prices of my favorite items had dropped. My username on both platforms was luke666, and I pretended to be a man. It was the only traceable online presence I had let myself maintain.

Silvia came to the table with a bottle of nebbiolo, and we started drinking. With the second glass, she loosened up and started talking about herself.

"It's not going well with Davide," she told me. "I think he's still seeing his ex."

I pretended to listen while I ate some peanuts. The combination of peanuts and wine created a singular flavor, much more interesting than Silvia's words were. Ever since I had begun the silence, Silvia's voice had sounded more petulant, or maybe the problem was that these days she talked about Davide a lot more. When she had a crush on someone, everything she talked about revolved around them, and after the first five minutes, it was difficult to feign interest. In that moment I was truly grateful to silence.

But what continued to surprise me was her inability to handle longer conversations, something that had never troubled her before. It had always been enough for her interlocutor to offer the occasional reaction—even just an *uh-huh* like you do on the phone to reassure the caller that the line hasn't dropped—and she was capable of monologizing for hours. Yet here she was now, tripping up after the first few sentences. Sometimes it made me feel disappointed; other times, it frightened me. She was going to grow tired of me eventually, and among the many likely consequences of silence, that was one possibility I had not yet considered. I saw her more like Bibi Andersson's character in *Persona*, someone who would hemorrhage words in the face of the total erasure of the other. But in some ways, her behavior was a credit to her. It was easy enough to paint her as an egocentric young woman who was more focused on satisfying her own wishes than on showing any interest toward others. She would never have admitted that my annihilation—as she would have described it—was a cause for concern. And yet it was. Silvia was faced with a problem, and she did not know how to solve it. The matter concerned someone other than herself, and she was not equipped to deal with it, like a guy who hasn't paid attention in his first aid course and now can only watch helplessly as his friend chokes. I felt sorry for her. Though I had stopped following what she was saying minutes ago, I looked up and tried to seem attentive, hoping she would stop stuttering. If I couldn't talk, I should at least practice listening. The fact that people were not as gripping as a Web search was not their fault.

"Are you listening to me?" said Silvia. "I hope so. I feel like I'm sitting in an empty confessional."

She wasn't going to ask me for advice anyway. And if she did, she wouldn't follow anything I suggested. So it didn't matter.

"The truth is," said Silvia, before another pause, "the truth is that I'm not as into him as I used to be. All the stuff he said to me, all those words I'd spent so long waiting for, they just don't mean the same anymore. They left me cold, and in the moment I thought it might be a temporary thing, to do with strong feelings—I can get like that sometimes. But then I got home and thought about it again, and again over the next few days, and still nothing. I just don't care like I used to. It's as if he spoke all those words in a foreign language, as if I understood their meaning but they didn't find their mark, if that makes sense."

I would have liked to know what those words had been. Why hadn't I listened properly? I tried to concentrate, but it was impossible to go back in time. Silvia finished her glass of wine and poured herself another, then topped me up to drain the bottle. I had begun to perceive the voices around me as a single soft entity, no longer annoying but comforting.

"I've never had that feeling before. I think it might be your fault," she said.

She did not clarify whether she thought this was a good thing or a bad thing. If it made her feel closer to me or if she hated me for sowing the seeds of doubt in her. Her expression did not point in either direction. She just looked at me for a moment, so that I was frozen, and after a silence, she returned to trivial topics. It occurred to me that even if I had been able to talk, I might not have asked her anything anyway, so perhaps this, too, was fine. There were millions of questions I had never asked because I was too scared to hear the answers, and the silence had given me an alibi, so that now I felt like less of a coward. As I pretended to listen, Silvia decided she was still hungry and that she wanted to sit on the sofa and eat a kebab while watching an episode of *Shameless*.

"Will you come with me?" she asked.

I didn't know if she meant to get a kebab or go home. So I simply followed her, and she did not object, and rather than feeling sorry for myself, as I might have done in different circumstances, I felt free. Without words getting in the way, making excuses or flaunting motivations, I could follow what my body and my mind wanted me to do. Silvia got me a kebab, too, and I tailed her like a pet dog. We went to her place and she turned on the TV without saying a word. She was already on season seven. I was still on the fifth.

I HAD STARTED having loads of dreams. In these dreams I spoke and people listened. Words flowed soft and unbidden from somewhere inside me—silk foulards, fresh milk, water from a mountain spring. My subconscious paid no heed to the idea of silence; it was as if nothing had changed. My mother, my father, Elena: they rarely appeared, but every time they did, they spoke to me—I don't recall what about—and I responded. One time I dreamt I was at their place for dinner—as if I still lived there, I think—and I was eating sweet fried semolina, a dish my mother never makes and that has no connection to the Modena area, where she is from, but that, due to some unexpected mechanism, coincides with one of my earliest memories. Maybe they served it for lunch at nursery school, or maybe it was at kindergarten, but now I would never know, as the only way to find out would have been to ask my mother.

Another time I dreamt that I was arguing with Silvia. In the dream we were in an empty room and I did not know about the silence, and all these horrible words kept coming out of my mouth, words I could not hold back. I told myself to stop, but every word seemed to trigger the next one, and the one after that was even worse. Silvia looked at me without reacting, moving her head slowly from right to left and back as if she were turning a thought over in her mind and trying to reposition it so that it would come into focus, or listening very closely to something and not wanting the left ear or vice versa to do all the work, and so putting the opposite ear forward to give the other one a reprieve. I kept vomiting words that cannot be repeated and thought that I must have gone mad, and that I ought to keep my mouth shut, so I looked for something to wedge between my teeth—a napkin, a pillow—but there was nothing in the room. I decided to bite my tongue, but it was not easy. It wriggled this way and that, and all I managed were glancing blows, which did not cut into it, but merely caused it to swell. I kept talking with my swollen tongue, I couldn't see Silvia anymore, but it didn't matter because all I could focus on was this living, pulsating thing that kept expanding and wanted to choke me. I was short of breath and wondering when I would find peace. Then I woke up.

Some mornings I felt sad and others I felt reinvigorated, and always simultaneously tired, like after having cried. I would get up and have a bath. I would plunge my head under the warm water and whisper random words, their sound covered by the still running tap. If I was in a hurry to get to work, I would have a shower instead, standing with my eyes closed and my mouth open, the pressure from the showerhead turned to the highest setting, the water hitting my skull so as to muffle sounds. *Shower, tower, flower.* I would swallow three times in a row to rehydrate my throat, then start again. *Yellow, mellow, fellow.* Unconnected words, words that communicated nothing, and the only thing they had in common was the sound they made. I liked words when they could be taken individually; they were graceful and harmonious. They were like people. *People, steeple, steerage.* Every time I swallowed my saliva, I felt a pain in my chest, beneath my sternum, in the spot where they say our heart resides.

From the kitchen window I could see the building across the street. When I got back home in the evenings, I would make myself an herbal tea and spy on the neighbors. I liked seeing what people get up to when they are alone, when they are practicing silence. My favorite was a guy in his fifties who smoked on his balcony in the dark, taking long drags that set the ashes at the tip of his cigarette alight, while the lampposts on the street altered the color of the sky, too purple to be real. He would finish his cigarette and stub it out on the table behind him, where he must have kept an ashtray, but he did not leave the stub there: he took it back inside, walking through the French doors into the living room and from there to the kitchen—to put the cigarette in the trash, I presumed. Then he would go back to the living room and read on the sofa or sit at the desk where he kept his computer. Ten or at most twenty minutes later he would go back out for another smoke, taking the same route to throw the cigarette away. I never saw him smoke during the daytime because he was out at work, while on the weekends he left before I woke up and stayed out until late, sometimes not returning until Sunday. If it was rainy he might stay at home, but he still never smoked before it got dark. He went to bed sometime between eleven and midnight, but I suspected he stayed up until much later, because the light from his bedroom stayed on until late. But there were no more smoking trips. I don't know what he did for work. I knew him through the hours he kept, as I didn't sleep either.

Another window I liked was the one on the floor below. This apartment was home to a woman in her seventies, probably widowed, who spent all of her time alone except for those three days in the week when she looked after her grandchildren. All boys—the eldest couldn't have been older than twelve—and all very lively. The lady would start cooking for them early in the morning, and after lunch she would sit them in front of the TV, putting on the programs they liked, while she returned to the kitchen and turned on the TV above the French doors, which opened onto the terrace. I could see what she was doing because although her windows, like everyone else's in the building, had curtains on them, she often kept them open, especially when her grandchildren were there, to let more light in. But when she retreated to the kitchen to watch her favorite shows—I pictured her tuning in to *Murder, She Wrote* or the courtroom reality show *Forum*, the same programs my grandmother watched whenever we ate together—she would draw the curtains so that she could see the screen better. Even on the coldest days, though, she would leave the window ajar, and when she cooked, a wisp of smoke would float out of that gap and mix with the wintry air. I saw her out on the street once: she had unusual features, and her skin, which must once have been extremely white, was papery and wrinkled, marked by time and by the sun. Small, elongated eyes, thin-tipped nose. A few days later I stopped to read the names on the intercom, and I was struck by a Nordic-sounding surname, or Dutch, perhaps, and thought it must be hers. Northern Europe had lent her an aversion to covering windows up, while from Italy she had inherited discretion and a sense of the value—or perhaps the comfort—of privacy. She did not talk to her grandchildren much, and I thought she must still be embarrassed about some inflection in her voice, sharp and metallic, that she couldn't quite erase or the occasional word she couldn't conjure, for in her mind and in her dreams, she still spoke Flemish.

I WAS ABLE to notice many more things than I had before, as if silence had sharpened my senses, the same way they say a dog's can be, or blind or deaf people's: to compensate. When I was little, I used to wonder why our voice was not considered one of the senses, and why, if our sensory organs are those that allow human beings to interact with others, the mouth was only included in relation to taste and not the spoken word. And also why, if the word was not one of the five senses, should mutism be considered by us kids to be among the three most terrifying conditions we might be afflicted with. *Would you rather be mute, deaf, or blind?* was the question you were inevitably asked. I used to reply that I would have chosen a different sense, one nobody cared about, like touch or at most smell, meaning that you would miss out on the smell of chocolate snacks and apricot shampoo but at least you'd also avoid stinky things. They told me that wasn't fair, it was too easy, so I would reply that I would have sacrificed hearing, because I did not want them to know the truth. They did not know that I was already devoted to a different kind of silence. A secret ambition I carried with me, sewn into the lining. Something for which there was no academic path to follow, but only—from one moment to the next—improvisation.

Gills

UNDER THE SYSTEM of binomial nomenclature, it is categorized as *Pterois volitans*, though it is more commonly known as scorpionfish, lionfish, or sometimes, in Italy, as flying scorpionfish.

Mine was called Harpo, though he was never going to know that, and not calling him by his name seemed to me the most respectful way of hosting an animal at home, albeit in captivity. But anyway, in my head, he was called Harpo. I had purchased him from an aquarium website for fifty-six euros. The tank, the accessories, the setup, and his food had cost more than twice that amount. But after two months of silence, I had earned this. A gift to myself to mark the date. Someone to share the silence with, as people like to say about elderly couples.

Harpo is a *Pterois volitans*, and like all *Pterois volitans*, he does not enjoy having other members of his species around. This is thought to explain why they tend to proliferate in more remote areas, where there are many kilometers to separate one scorpionfish from the next. Early on, as soon as they become self-sufficient, the younger fish leave their families behind in search of new habitats. In this, Harpo and I differed. But I could learn from him.

Another of the peculiarities of the *Pterois volitans* is that it is venomous. It possesses a total of sixteen venomous spines—thirteen dorsal spines and three anal spines—which protect it from potential dangers. Its venom is deadly to other aquatic creatures but unlikely to kill humans, though it can produce symptoms ranging from ecchymosis to necrosis and vomiting, and from breathing difficulties to pulmonary edema and syncope. None of this stops people from eating these fish, partly because of their delectable taste, and partly as a means of population control. For despite its aversion to social contact, the scorpionfish has an extremely high fertility rate, and is thus considered an invasive species. Especially in the Caribbean, where it is said to have had devastating effects on biodiversity.

It can live comfortably in an aquarium, though, so long as it is provided with hiding places. I bought Harpo a rock with a crevice he could squeeze into. And squeeze into it he did. He would spend half the day in there, virtually invisible. I pictured him sleeping there. (Do fish sleep?) He would reemerge toward the evening. I fed him on alternate days: dried crustaceans, krill, tiny frozen fish. I would defrost them in hot water and dangle them in front of him with a pair of tweezers, moving them back and forth to spark his predatory instincts, like people do with cats. Every now and then I would reward him with fresh shrimp or small, live fish. He appreciated this. The scorpionfish is a superpredator that feeds on a wide variety of sea creatures and sometimes even on smaller members of its own species. The more I learned about him, the prouder I felt. Harpo would devour everything I gave him to eat, then start swimming in circles. I envisioned the digestive system inside that armored, unpleasant little body, a living danger signal that nature had equipped with superior tools to act as a warning to the creatures around him and encourage members of his own species to keep their distance.

I had placed the fish tank on a piece of IKEA furniture that had come with the apartment, next to the window in the living room, so that the sunlight streaming in would be refracted onto the walls of the room. Come sunset, the whole place looked like a giant kaleidoscope. I would lie on the sofa and watch the aquarium instead of the TV, and then look at the walls, at the frenzied traffic of tiny colored diamonds chasing one another, hummingbirds, rainbows, crystals. I tried to follow them with my gaze but it wasn't easy, little soap bubbles bursting silently and without a trace. They seemed like people to me, each with their own journey and to-do list. They seemed like people when they are placed within a social context, not when they are alone. People who have a purpose. People who find a purpose, even if it is just buying a pint of milk or some toilet paper. When they return to their homes, they disappear from our sight and go back to being themselves, tiny nonentities teeming with thoughts, unable to comprehend their own nature or their reason. That is why I liked to spy on them from the window as they walked on the street below. Like wandering ectoplasms.

Harpo had no purpose other than to be a fish, a solitary fish, and he would spend his days between his rock and the rest of the fish tank, floating aimlessly from one side to the other. Sometimes I wondered if he could see me and if he thought of me as a total stranger, a four-tentacled giant who held him captive and fed him, or if he was merely embarrassed by my constant staring and tried, when he was awake and out of his den, to find something to do. I wondered about this because there was no way I would ever know the answer.

Nothing about him ever communicated his intentions. He did not communicate with me, and therefore he could not communicate with anyone else, because none of his fellow fish could see him. It's the classic example of the tree that falls in an empty forest: no one could hear Harpo = Harpo did not make a sound. He was the perfect animal with whom to share my condition, the only living being who would not be continually reminding me of the choice I'd made, who would not challenge it or make me feel like a constant disappointment.

Murphy, my parents' dog, would have followed me around looking for praise, for a gesture, getting excited over what little crumbs I might toss him and growing depressed if I ignored him. If I stood before him without making a sound, Murphy would start to whine and hover around me with his eyes wide open, seeking my attention with the same voracious appetite with which he requested food from my mother. He would plead for my father's praise too, knowing that the most he was going to get was a pat on the head, as swift and frictionless as those claw machines in arcades, the ones with which you are supposed to fish stuffed toys out of a pile but that usually end up just giving your prize a fleeting, insolent brush. At this point my mother would inevitably say what she always said: *Come on, talk to him.* She had conditioned Murphy just as she had conditioned us, with an alternating pattern of praise and abuse that had turned him into a bona fide member of the family. But there were a couple of things Murphy knew he could count on: food, twice a day (at seven in the morning and seven in the evening), and the short walk right before, which my mother saved for herself no matter what—her moment of solitude and contemplation at the beginning and end of each day.

Murphy was a rescue we'd acquired when I was twenty years old and Elena was twenty-five and still living with us. She'd been the one to find him and persuade our parents to take him in, despite their insistence, throughout our childhood, that they would not allow pets in the house. But it had been a difficult year: first our grandfather—my mother's father—had died, and then my father had been diagnosed with a tumor. A very small mass in his brain that had turned out to be benign, but he'd still had to go through surgery and treatment and all the rest of it. Once he'd recovered, my sister had taken my mother to one side and told her that we wanted to give him a present—she'd used the plural even though it had been her idea—to cheer him up and to show him that we loved him and stood by him. Something that was not exactly material in nature, and would require nurturing and companionship. Something that would basically tell him: You're not going anywhere.

Our mother kept repeating that animals ought to roam free in the countryside, not be locked up in the house—a house that, on top of everything else, they might soil and scratch and fill with fur—but Elena had eventually managed to convince her that we should get a dog. They'd argued about it for ages; my mother was not one to concede quickly—someone like her wouldn't even let illness break her resistance—but eventually she had caved. She had *very slowly* caved, her surrender the fruit of an incalculable effort practiced day by day, an exercise in habituation. I had watched her examining the space around her to evaluate whether it was dog-proof, moving furniture around, creating little nooks, storing fragile objects away, even just in her imagination. She would stop and stare at a corner, at a room, and that was how I was able to tell that she was changing. She had observed the space before her and I had observed her, wondering if she had gone through the same process when they had decided to have children, if she had started wanting us the moment she had begun to look at space in a different way, if that was the way she had first begun to look after us.

I had done the same with Harpo, which was proof that I too was capable of taking care of someone. That the silence bore no relation to coldness.

Harpo reciprocated in his own way, eating the food I gave him and hiding in the nooks I had provided for him. I didn't need anything else. I wouldn't ask him for anything else. I was determined not to. I have always looked upon the behavior of dogs with suspicion and reproach, their inexhaustible need for attention, impossible to satisfy, filling me with tenderness every time and making me feel—every time—insufficient and inadequate. Harpo needed nothing but his shrimp and his space. But when he looked at me through the glass sometimes, floating in the middle of the tank—I liked to think he was watching me—he reminded me of certain kinds of children, those who are a little more mature than average, possessing excellent verbal capabilities but little inclination to put them into practice—those kids who meet your gaze and stand there, still and silent and staring, until you realize they've figured you out.

It was precisely this doggishness of Murphy's that my mother had grown to love, as well as the fact that he was especially so with her, even though out of all of us, she was the one who least expected to receive affection from him, who never demanded it and rarely showed it, yet always got it in return. Dogs can be like that, growing attached to whoever pets them the least, just like some people do. In that absence they see purpose, a kind of motivation; they devote their existence to persuasion, continually seeking to close the distance. Murphy would wait patiently for my mother to come back from work, always sitting in the same spot, and her arrival was his reward. I saw something of my father in him. Or, at least, that was how he was jokingly portrayed by everyone else, by people outside the family—by their mutual friends. My father appeared as a sedate, docile being at the mercy of my mother's hardness, my mother, who was kind and attentive toward him only when there was nobody to witness it. Not even then, in truth. But I knew that they spoke a secret language, had a sustained and discreet manner of renewing their reciprocal vows. These were imperceptible things: a reference to some shared experience of which we only knew the rough outline; a joke followed by a quick glance of amusement at some flaw or blunder; some annoying but inconsequential trait they tolerated in each other. Scattered over an ocean of daily gestures, these were small, fleeting movements that Elena and I had learned to recognize—unbeknownst to them, and unbeknownst to each other. And they reassured us every time.

In a similar way, Murphy and my mother cultivated a whole pattern of daily gestures that modestly and delicately reflected their fondness for each other. When she woke up in the night to use the toilet, she never failed to visit him in the living room—to which he was confined, not being allowed into the bedrooms—and give his head a scratch, standing in the half-light from the lampposts outside and not even turning the lights on. Apart from them, I was the only one who knew of this ritual, which I had witnessed one sleepless night when, no longer able to tolerate my bedroom, I had gone into the kitchen, then nearly fallen asleep on the sofa, until suddenly—with my eyes better accustomed to the darkness than hers—I had seen my mother stroking Murphy's snout, murmuring *Good dog, good dog* as if she were reciting a psalm, and I had lain there, holding my breath as I watched them, praying I would not be seen, vowing never to go into that room at night again, vowing to let them be.

March

SILVIA AND I went out again a couple of times. It wasn't at all easy. It worked better when there was loads of background noise, but alcohol made everything tougher. When we were around other people, I kept having to rein in that part of the brain that controls the tongue, which sometimes felt like it didn't even belong to me. I kept drinking to avoid thinking about it, and the result was that I couldn't think about anything at all, including what I was doing and why, and the whole endeavor suddenly seemed stupid and juvenile and senseless, a spoiled child refusing to eat their vegetables. So one night I decided to stop. We were in the same bar where we had spent New Year's Eve. That felt like a lifetime ago. We were sitting on one of the sofas; I was next to Silvia, who was talking about something that had happened to us years before when we had responded to a job listing and found ourselves at a Herbalife meeting. But Silvia, whose memory was terrible, kept altering loads of details and omitting others that I knew to be important. Like the way the lady who had posted the job listing had addressed us as if she already owned us, and tried to persuade us to enter into the pyramid scheme with the wild-eyed look of someone who's taken too many drugs. Silvia recalled how they had persuaded us to try some of the concoctions they publicized, and claimed that when we had left, I had vomited into a trash can. But actually she had been the one to vomit, not me.

I was sitting right there, yet I couldn't correct her, I couldn't offer my version of events, and I felt stupid. I'm sure that's the impression I gave, from the outside: a pretty face with nothing to say, an empty brain. The previous week, Silvia had told her friends about the choice I had made, and her friends had bombarded me with questions.

"This is crazy," they'd said. "Are you sure it's not some kind of vow?"

"Have you been recruited by a cult? Blink twice for yes."

Silvia laughed, and I forced myself to do the same. Fabio was the only one who didn't ask me anything. "I admire her," he said. He had a rather loud voice and did not have to struggle to make himself heard over the music. "I hate words. The best relationship I ever had was with a Croatian guy. He didn't speak a word of Italian or English. Four months of pure sex, no arguments—it was heaven. I have never felt so much affinity with another person."

"Why did it end?" asked one of Silvia's friends.

"He started learning Italian."

Silvia, on the other hand, was embarrassed. I could sense her resentment in the way she avoided looking at me, unlike the others, who peered at me as if I were some wounded animal lying on the side of the road. The aura of resentment and embarrassment she emanated was so thick it frightened me. I thought she must regret having invited me. I couldn't exactly blame her.

After the Herbalife anecdote, she went back to talking about herself. "The supplements that some companies send me and ask me to post about aren't that different, actually," she said. "But at least they get the job done. I'll never be constipated again. What goes in will come out."

The attention was back on her now, and I felt relieved of the burden of the others' gazes. Now that they had started laughing at her jokes and stopped laughing at me, I could feel my body gradually thawing. I got up, went to the bathroom, looked in the mirror. The fluorescent lights gave me a mystical appearance, and I saw myself as an ordinary girl who was agonizing over something that did not exist, who was inflicting some idiotic torture upon herself, wearing a hair shirt that, instead of freeing her as she had thought it would, pained her and weighed her down even more. How foolish it was to try to evade the impositions of institutions and of society by creating other ones to bow to; I might as well have joined a cult or become an anti-vaxxer or stepped into the endlessly labyrinthine world of ethical non-monogamy. I might as well have joined Herbalife, back then. All I had done was to change the prefix of my actions, but the effect was the same: no redemption, only a series of new restrictions. A new and weighty label to try to pass off as a choice made freely. This, my dear, I told myself as I stood there a handspan from the mirror, the outline of my face blurring away, this is what everyone does, even as they remain explicitly convinced of their difference.

I walked out of the bathroom feeling certain that I was going to put an end to it. I sat down among the others and thought: Now I'm going to say something. Then it happened. I couldn't do it. My tongue, which had spent the whole evening trying not to respond to my commands, was now genuinely unresponsive. I tried again, but nothing. I couldn't talk. I was past the pain threshold. I had succeeded in my quest.

Silvia kept drinking and prattling on to her friends, her voice very loud to overcome the music, and squeaky from all the drinks she'd had. Many times I pondered whether to leave, but the same force that prevented me from speaking was also stopping me from getting up from the sofa. But when Silvia was sufficiently drunk, she dragged me to the bar, where she ordered a Moscow mule for herself and a gin and tonic for me, remembering to ask for Hendrick's instead of Gordon's, and said: "I hate you, Martinez. Why does everything have to be so complicated."

Then she gave me a wet kiss on the cheek and started dancing. I was dancing too, with the strange sensation that the silence enabled me to hear the music better. Like having tiny vibrations under the skin demanding to be let out through movement. But maybe it was just the effects of the alcohol in addition to the joint I had smoked before going out. It was to be the last time I went to that place with Silvia.

DANIELE CAME TO visit me every Friday, as we had agreed. The last day I was still speaking, I had requested that we see each other weekly. A week between one meeting and the next seemed to me an adequate length of time for us both. He had suggested Friday nights, pizza, and a movie at home, as if we were still in high school. I had agreed, thinking he would soon tire of it all, but in fact he seemed to possess superhuman reserves of patience. I wondered if he would agree with Fabio, if in a few years' time he would remember this as the happiest relationship he'd ever been in.

On the first day after the start of the silence, he'd brought over a DVD for us to watch together. He now brought a couple every week, on loan from the library if they were classics or purchased at the supermarket if they were more recent releases.

I was enchanted by the tenderness of the gesture, his need to indulge me, mixed with a romantic and slightly outdated penchant for resisting progress. Giacomo would have turned up with a USB stick or even with his own external hard drive containing an impressive catalog of torrents downloaded from websites he checked every day. But Giacomo's tastes were more refined, while Daniele, who relied purely on instinct, almost always brought me films I had seen at least three times already or heavily publicized new commercial releases, which often tended to be boring and banal, the kind of film you watch on a Sunday afternoon or on a Saturday night at the multiplex. Still, every now and then he got it right. I behaved exactly as I had done with Giacomo: when a movie managed to rise above mediocrity and also went beyond just being *all right*, it became something that was not be shared, but to be handled with care and pondered in solitude and silence. The only difference was that obviously silence was now the treatment every film received, regardless of its worth.

Daniele always brought two DVDs, because after watching the first movie, we would have sex—on the sofa, in the bedroom, or on the kitchen table, from where I sometimes caught sight of Harpo and wondered if he understood what was happening—then smoke a cigarette and move on to the next film. Sometimes we felt like doing it again, and when it was over we would sit there, holding our cigarettes, with Daniele struggling to fill the silence. It was a beautiful moment: the absence of conversation, which—even after the first few times—always tended to be empty, and the embarrassment exuding from his slender, naked body and expressed in ungainly gestures and little coughs, an embarrassment that you could almost smell, and that I found intoxicating, though I did not know why. I began to notice that he was talking more and more, and each time his stories became longer and more confident, as if he had been rehearsing them in front of the mirror at home, as if he was really trying. I wasn't sure whether he was doing it for me or for himself, but I enjoyed seeing him put all that effort into filling the emptiness, bringing order to that oversized space.

"Can I feed Harpo?" he would ask. "I guess so . . . Or maybe you've already fed him? Well, anyway, I suppose a few more krill won't hurt, right?"

The first time Daniele saw the fish tank, he was as excited as a child. "I love aquariums! But where are all the fish?" Harpo had gone into hiding as soon as he had heard Daniele come in, but after a few minutes, he had reappeared. "How strange," Daniele said. "I've never seen one like this." He'd taken Harpo's photo and checked online to figure out what species he belonged to. After that he'd looked up some information on how to care for him, what to feed him, and his life expectancy. "Ten years! Not bad for a fish, eh?"

"He's got a face like a piranha, don't you think? You look like a cannibal, buddy. But all you're going to get are these little shrimp."

I was thinking that if I could have spoken, I would have corrected him and told him that the term he should have used was *anthropophagus*, but yes, Harpo really was a cannibal, because if he had been living out in the wild, he would also have eaten other members of his own species. You're so *pedantic*, my mother would have said. I could still feel my stomach burn every time I felt the urge to speak, and I was convinced it must be the same acid I would normally inject into my responses. Truly, this silence was less of a gift to myself than it was to other people.

"Do you ever spy on your neighbors? You can see everything from here. I'm always tempted to do it."

He was getting better and better: fewer questions, mostly rhetorical, or to which he promptly replied himself.

"The other night I went out for dinner to a really nice Japanese restaurant that's just opened. I remember you told me you like Asian food. We could go there next week. We don't always have to meet here. It's not like you're sick or anything. I could order for you. It'll be fun, right? I could end up ordering stuff you hate, or I might guess correctly. Here's what we'll do: it's Easter next week and I'll be away with my parents. So we won't see each other on Friday. But the Friday after that, if you're up for it, I'll come and pick you up at eight and you can be dressed to go out. It's not that I mind seeing you in your tracksuit, I was just thinking it would be . . . like a sign, I suppose. The first that came into my head."

He was less controlled when he was nervous.

"Guess who I ran into on my way here? Silvia. She was going over to her parents' place —they live nearby. I didn't know that. She asked me what I was doing around here and so I . . . well, I told her we're seeing each other. Should I not have said anything? Does it bother you? Oh, right, sorry. Well, I hope I didn't make a mistake. She asked how you were doing, said she's going to come by and visit you soon."

I was pretty sure she wasn't going to. She hadn't reached out all week, and she was due to go to Tuscany the next day for a photo shoot. A really terrible swimwear brand, she'd said, the kind where the stuff that gets delivered to your house doesn't even remotely look like the pictures on the website, but she was bleeding her bank account dry and needed the money. Suddenly I missed the way she smelled, and I tried to banish the feeling by focusing on something else. I started staring at the nape of Daniele's neck while he fiddled with the DVD player and put *Limitless* on. It occurred to me that I wouldn't mind having a nape like that by my side for the rest of my life, for if in Silvia's case it was her scent that I missed, this was the part of Daniele's body I thought about the most during the rest of the week. I realized that I was thinking so hard about it that he might notice, and I would thus violate the pact and break the vow I had made, as well as betray every other pride-related moral obligation I had put in place ever since I had first learned how to reason. Suddenly I felt like I was back in a cage. I looked at Harpo and concentrated on the movie, which I had already seen years ago, though Daniele would never know.

When the movie was over we fucked on the sofa. Sex was the only time I could truly be myself, which is what I thought as I straddled him and he followed my lead. All the rest of the time, I was totally compliant. I passively accepted everyone else's decisions, I couldn't respond to any remarks I didn't agree with, I didn't correct anyone. But during sex I could say my piece, using my body and communicating nothing but desire. In this I felt at peace. I wasn't betraying anybody. I was an atheist nun who practiced nothing but silence. No devotion, no abstinence from carnal pleasures. I was no different from any other animal.

Afterward we always smoked and he was not as bold as before and more respectful of the silence. We would watch the smoky phantoms floating away from us, and sometimes I would lean against his chest. I could hear his heart beating and would try to figure out if it was going any faster, if my presence had any kind of effect on him. Silvia had once told me that Davide's heart always beat faster when she hugged him, and that seemed to her a more honest expression than most words or material gestures could ever be.

At a certain point I realized Daniele's breathing had become heavier, and when I turned to look at him, I saw that he had fallen asleep. It was the first time this had happened, and I did not know how to interpret it. I moved off his chest and fidgeted a little, hoping he would wake up, but he was fast asleep. So I leaned against a pillow and waited. I tried not to stare at him too much. Watching someone sleep felt like a scene from a movie, something silly and a little cloying. And I was afraid of falling in love. In *Dawson's Creek*, Pacey realizes he has fallen in love with Joey when he stays up all night to watch her sleep. It sounds really creepy when you put it that way, but back when we were teenagers, it was what we all would have wanted. That's another problem with words, I thought. All those instances when a thing loses its value after it is spoken aloud. Whereas in darkness, wrote someone I couldn't remember, the treasure continues to shine. Darkness was going to protect me from the unwitting violence of words. Feelings, it seemed to me, are raw nerves and exposed flesh.

I tried to go to sleep, but it wasn't easy. I could hear Daniele's breathing, which felt like an alien presence, come to ruin the peace I had worked so hard to carve out for myself. If I turned away, I couldn't see him and it was like having Giacomo behind me. What did I do before, when I was in bed with someone and couldn't fall asleep? I felt the urge to go on social media, check to see how the world was moving forward without me. I missed the women I used to follow on Instagram, the stories people posted, the photos in front of the mirror, the sponsored content they didn't tag. I missed the comments beneath the posts from the daily newspapers, the ungrammatical outpourings of frustrated and lonely individuals who were afraid of the slightest hint of progress, afraid of diversity, angry at both the rich and powerful and the weak, angry at wealth and destitution, incapable of getting through to the end of an article and sometimes even of deciphering a headline, lacking in logical and reading-comprehension skills; I missed everything that had driven me to being the way I was now. It had been an egotistical, conceited kind of drive, but it was also what had defined me, had convinced me that I was better than them. An impulse that occasionally needed rekindling.

But I lacked the motivation, now. I lacked it more in this moment than ever before, now that temptation took the form of a warm and pulsating body, another's breath breaking the silence, penetrating my eardrums and my lungs, intoxicating me and persuading me that everything was fine. Tenderness is the cruelest form of torture. There is no training in the world that can prepare you for it. So I grabbed Daniele's phone, unlocked it with the code I had seen him enter a long time ago, opened Instagram, and immersed myself in something I hadn't done in months. I immediately searched for the influencers I used to follow most closely, as if they were old friends I hadn't heard from in a while. I put headphones on and watched their stories, then their highlights, their reels, their posts. I tried to spot every change that had occurred since I had last seen them: the cut and color of their hair, their choice of outfits, their regular themed posts, their travel, the products they sponsored. Some of them had new pets, new children, new homes. The things that sparked their outrage were different. There were new things they sought to normalize. Sadness, apathy, seasonal depression, their job, feeling tired from working too much, feeling gratified for working too much, a lack of maternal instinct, an excess of maternal instinct. Everything was to be normalized. They posted photos from the airport and quizzed their followers—"Where am I headed?"—or they posted a question box saying, "Ask me anything <3." They gave irritated responses as they walked down the street or lay in bed. The stories that followed were screenshots of messages from their followers, who either agreed with them or insulted them. I opened YouTube, onto the current affairs, entertainment, and culture accounts. *An American couple has decided to name their child They and not assume their gender until the child decides. What do you think?* View all 1,359 comments. I kept this up for over an hour, always ready to drop the phone every time Daniele so much as moved or there was any change in the frequency or the timbre of his breathing. I kept going until I recognized the return of a familiar feeling, a subtle but pervasive rage, a visceral disgust that swept away all traces of melancholy.

The last thing I did was to check Silvia's profile to see how many more followers and how many more posts she'd added since we'd last been in touch, where she had been and with whom. There were only two active stories on her profile: one was a photo she had taken in a lift, dressed all in black and with her hood pulled up, above the caption *Be right back, off to rob a bank*, and the other was San Carlo Square in blazing sunlight and a caption that said, *Drunkenness level: crossing San Carlo Square on our hands and feet, full bridge pose*. I'd been there that evening. I was still convinced that Silvia was a better person in real life.

I put the phone down and savored nothingness again, before I too fell asleep. I slept deeply until the morning, as if I hadn't slept in months. Maybe I hadn't. Without my even realizing it, the fact of having somebody beside me, someone to share the air that came out of my lungs, carbon dioxide mixing with oxygen, had quieted a part of me that was always vigilant, still yet alert, like an animal in captivity. I woke up toward midday, alone, because Daniele always knew the right thing to do, and so he had left. He had written me a note, which he had placed on the kitchen table. *I'm sorry, I fell asleep*, it said. *I'll see you the Friday after next. Remember: if you want to go for dinner, make sure you're dressed to go out, and wearing shoes. Whichever ones you want, I don't mind what you choose. I don't mind what you wear, I'm always into you.*

I spent a few seconds wondering if his use of anaphora was intentional, as it sounded pretty great. I realized that it had been a while since I'd read anything and I was no longer used to the voice in my head that pronounced words in my stead, and that sounded a lot like my own—at least the voice other people could hear. It took me a moment to actually take in the meaning of his words, and when I did, they elicited a fluttering in my stomach, or in my heart—somewhere in that region, anyhow. Had spending one night together been enough to change everything? I thought about it all week, and it was the longest week since the start of the silence.

IN THE FACULTY LIBRARY, with rustling pages and soft, murmuring voices in the background, I asked myself if he had done it on an impulse, maybe still feeling a little tipsy from the night before, or if he had planned it. I had been asleep in the meantime, and the idea that he had watched me while he wrote his note, sat there in front of me in a way I could not control, filled me with fear and embarrassment. I had fallen asleep like a deaf dog, except my ears worked perfectly fine. There's never been a case of a mute person whose condition has led them to sleeping more deeply than the average person, yet there I was. I wished

I had the note with me, so I could continue to analyze it and examine his handwriting, try to guess whether he'd scribbled it in a rush, if he'd thought twice about any of it. Maybe he'd written it without thinking too much, emboldened by the knowledge that I would not be able to respond to him. Except I was going to respond. That was what he didn't understand. Getting ready to go out with him and accepting his invitation would be a response. But the same would be true of not getting ready, of waiting for him in sweatpants and slippers. Either way, it would be something. And he had put me in a corner. Without even realizing what he'd done.

Or maybe . . . or maybe I had misinterpreted the note and none of this meant very much to him. He was another one of those people to whom words didn't really matter that much. They just used them like this, indiscriminately, negating any kind of exclusivity. If that was the case, would I consider it a betrayal? The answer was yes. The worst kind of betrayal? How important was it for other people to be like me? I realized that I did not know how to respond to that question. My views alternated with each passing day: sometimes I felt like I could forgive a murderer as long as he agreed with me, and sometimes I loathed myself so much that I ended up detesting anyone in whom I saw any reflection of my own inclinations.

I missed Giacomo's composure, his imperturbability, that divine capacity he had for always remaining the way he was, and how honest he was not to hide it. Daniele came across as inscrutable at times, as if he were locked in a constant battle between what he would have liked to do and what he couldn't do. Or perhaps he was merely taking advantage of the situation and using me as his guinea pig, readying himself for the big match, for a more important future relationship. I could just picture him going after a stable, clean, reassuring woman he could show off to his family and friends, someone I certainly couldn't be. Depending on the day, I blamed either his Catholic education or a lack of remorse.

That's how the week went by, without my being able to pick between the two. When I was home I couldn't relax, so I practiced what had become my favorite sport ever since Elena had introduced me to that world and I had turned it into an art: endlessly browsing real estate websites to look at houses I was never going to live in. I could do this for hours without registering the passage of time, only noticing, perhaps, when my eyes began to burn. I would start off with the higher-budget listings, the kinds of homes I would never be able to afford. Houses with swimming pools, panoramic views, gyms, and cinema rooms. I scrolled through the photos and looked at how they were furnished. I was obsessed with kitchens; the bigger they were, the greater my appreciation. Then I homed in on the details: I was particularly interested in doors and parquet floors. I knew every kind of wood there was: teak, maple, ash, *wenge, iroko, doussie. Afromosia, sapele, okoumé*.

From the more expensive listings I would move on to the more economical ones. I would criticize the owners for the predictability of their choices, while I was always looking for the unexpected—the kind of furniture that was so tawdry and inappropriate, the kind of choices that were so uncomfortable and ill-conceived that they ended up feeling like works of genius. Once I found an apartment with a toilet in the living room; another time I saw a kitchen fully fitted with mirrored cupboards, like in a dance studio. The final step, after which I was usually tired enough to go to sleep, was to filter the search results by *Price: lowest to highest*. Now the first few pages of listings were little more than hovels. The furniture was recycled, the layouts claustrophobic. Sometimes the height of the ceiling was below the legal limit. These places were often rented on the black market. All things considered, I had been lucky to find my apartment.

Once I had gone through all the worst listings, I would oscillate between euphoria and unease. I felt like a better person than the kinds of people who charged disproportionate rents for houses with crooked furniture, houses whose stink of mildew you could practically see in the photos; and I felt more fortunate than the kinds of people who were forced to live in those places. But soon I couldn't help but picture myself inside one of those apartments: a stifling attic with the sun blazing into it, a bed wedged into a corner, bedcovers hiding the stained mattress gone yellow from the sweat of past tenants, cheap paneling on the walls. I saw myself lying on that bed, living on candy and crisps and cigarettes consumed all at once, desperately seeking out the oxygen that had squeezed through the only window in the room—a transom placed over the bed, sucking carbon monoxide out of the room and returning it at a ratio of three to one—and rationing my breathing just as I did my words.

April

Two days later it was Easter and I was forced to have lunch with my parents. It was a nice day, the weather was getting warmer, and I decided to walk to Porta Nuova station to catch a bus from there. When I got to the station, I looked at my watch and saw that it was still early, so I proceeded on foot. Once you were out of the city center, there were fewer people around; they strolled alone or in pairs, walking their dogs, wearing sunglasses, their coats unbuttoned. Cars drove by at an appropriate distance from one another. The wild brambles along the river Dora had started flowering a few days before—I'd noticed on my way to work and had felt like I was walking through a snow globe, one with pink petals falling instead of snowflakes. The trees were beginning to grow leaves again, a gloomy red tending to brown, or so it seemed to me through the dark lenses of my glasses. There were still a few petals left behind. Elsewhere, bushes in full bloom, yellow and white. Nature's springtime insolence had always frightened me and made me anxious, but this time it was different. Silence had made me more alert, more receptive to my senses and to stimuli, but also less vulnerable. It was a smooth and pleasurable sensation, like slipping under fresh bedsheets when you've just shaved your legs. The world bothered me less.

This would come in handy for getting through lunch. My mother had invited her brother, Paolo, whom neither Elena nor I ever addressed as uncle because ever since we were little, he himself had always forbidden us from doing so. During the summers, which we used to spend camping all together or in one of the holiday apartments my father rented for us, Paolo would hide our toys. He was convinced it was funny, though he was the only one laughing. My mother would wince; my father would shake his head and leave the room. One day, Elena and I decided to have our revenge by hiding his box of extremely valuable cigars and his golden lighter, and we did it so well that neither of these items was ever found again. This episode did have some negative consequences—my mother punished us by forbidding us to go to the beach for two days—but it had positive ones too, in that it earned us our uncle's respect and led to him granting us a truce.

For years we tolerated one another without much thought—that is, until Paolo began to claim that the most effective cure for cancer was aloe vera extract, that the mind could control the body, and that vaccinations caused autism. His new partner had a daughter from her previous marriage. It had been a home birth, a so-called lotus birth—although that pleasant word prettified a rather stomach-turning practice. Briefly put, the umbilical cord is not cut at birth; the placenta and other fetal matter thus remain attached to the newborn, who carries them for days until they detach of their own accord. Paolo and his partner described the process to us over lunch at my parents' house one day, and my mother, who had just bitten into a morsel of sausage stew, let slip a heartfelt "That's disgusting." Elena and I burst out laughing, but my uncle's partner did not take it so well. It was the last time she came round. But since he was not allowed to join any festivities involving the family of the father of the lotus-birthed child, our mother regularly invited him to join us instead. "He's still my brother," she would say with a shrug. And he regularly accepted her invitations.

I rang my parents' doorbell, and my mother opened the door without asking who it was. A habit that long predated the silence, and that I had always found to be reassuring.

"There you are," said Elena as she set the table. "Will you give me a hand?"

Elia was playing on a blanket on the floor. Car-shaped wooden cubes. *Isn't he a little too old for this stuff?*, I might have asked. My parents and I had gifted him a mini Ferrari for his third birthday, but Elena still insisted on giving him the wooden versions designed for toddlers.

Marco had already sat down and was nibbling on some bread. "Who's missing?" he asked.

"Paolo," my mother replied. "He's on his way."

Paolo was always late. It was one of the rare things about him that I appreciated, because it made me look punctual. My sister sat Elia at the table and placed in front of him a bowl containing a small portion of the same agnolotti the rest of us would soon also eat. Elia was not a great fan of stuffed pasta, and after a while he started spitting the food back out onto his plate. My sister was in the middle of telling our parents about an argument she'd had at work, so by the time she noticed, it was too late. I stared at him as he showed me the mush in his mouth, as if to dare me. *You're disgusting*, I would have told him. He would have laughed. He went crazy for the word *disgusting*; I did not understand if it was due to the way it sounded or because of what it meant. I used to say it on purpose, just to amuse him.

"Why don't you talk anymore?" he'd asked me once. I'd made a funny face at him.

"Don't you know how to talk?" he'd kept needling. I'd pretended to wring his neck.

He asked me questions all the time ("What's this?" "Why don't you sleep here anymore?" "How old are you?" "What does it mean to 'whine'?"), just to put me to the test. I was the only one he asked, no one else, and it had begun precisely with the silence. Sometimes Elena would come to my rescue, distracting him or asking him to stop. "You know your aunt is not going to respond," my mother would interject. But there were also times when nobody said anything, and his questions were left there, suspended, filling up the room.

Finally Paolo arrived, and we all sat at the table. "No thanks," he told my mother when she offered him a plate of the agnolotti with a meaty sauce. "I've stopped eating meat. Only temporarily—I'm not really a vegetarian. I don't think I could do it. But Benedetta says it's good for the stomach. And for the head. You know I've always had migraines."

Benedetta was his partner, the one who'd gone for the placenta birth. Even her name—which meant "blessed"—was an affront. Her parents must either be zealous Catholics or have held extremely high expectations of their daughter. Which of course explained—at least in part—her "belated rebellion," as Silvia might have called it.

"Do you want some?" said Elia, offering me a forkful of puree. I shook my head. "Yes or no," he said. "It's good manners to reply to a question."

I took a mouthful of puree from my plate, turned toward him, and pushed the food through my teeth, with my jaws clenched shut and my lips curled up. "You're disgusting," he tried to say. He still couldn't quite pronounce the word properly.

"Leave her alone, darling," said Paolo. "It can't be easy for her. You know I still dream of cigarettes sometimes? But ever since I stopped smoking, I can see better. I almost don't need glasses anymore. Not to mention the karma, of course. Quitting smoking and not drinking cow's milk are the two things that have helped me the most. Oh, and clarified butter. Do you still use normal butter, Lea? I don't. It's crap. It's not surprising that people in India stopped using it many centuries ago."

He filled his mouth with puree, then turned to look at me. "Benedetta thinks it's a great idea, this word detox you're doing. She did it too, at a retreat many years ago. But it was only for a week. She really admires you. You know you're alkalinizing your body, right? Your cells will thank you for it."

I caught Elena's eye and saw that she had secretly been looking at me. My father, too, could barely withhold his laughter. *Thank you very much*, I would have told them.

"The important thing is to not stray too far from emotions. To make sure you don't leave empathy behind. All the great psychopaths are like this. Though of course they descend from reptiles."

"The great psychopaths?" said Marco, who loved to provoke him.

"The new world order. The crooked elites."

"And what have lizards got to do with any of that?"

"Don't you know? There have been studies about this. All the great psychopaths of this earth have different genes than the rest of us. It's likely that their DNA was mixed with that of alien reptiles. Some people say they might even be aliens themselves, capable of taking human form. I don't know, I'm not sure whether I believe that part yet. But for sure they're not human. Reptiles don't feel emotions like we do, you know. They are not genetically predisposed toward empathy. That's why they are capable of eating their young, and things like that."

"But other animals do that too, don't they?" said Marco, forcing a cough to avoid laughing. "What have you got against reptiles?"

"I'm not making this up," said Paolo, sounding peeved. "It's a fact that reptiles don't feel emotions in the same way mammals do. There have been studies about it. Look online."

I remembered that dream I'd had months before in which I was a lizard or an iguana or perhaps a snake. All I could recall was the scaly skin and the sensation of my tongue being thinner than normal, the feel of my belly against the earth. I wondered what I would have done if I had still been able to talk. Maybe I would have told Paolo about the dream, just to goad him, and I would have convinced him that I was a shapeshifter. My mother would have had to intervene.

I could be like that sometimes: I would get fired up and start raising my voice and talking really fast, hoping to prove some kind of theory. It was the same kind of hope that inflamed Paolo and all those other people who thought the sorts of things he thought. Sometimes I said things that were mean or too personal, too cutting, thus losing all credibility and ending up on the wrong side of the argument. But that day all I felt was a kind of warmth in my chest, controlled and totally pleasant, which allowed me to forget that previously, and not that long ago, I had been entirely dominated by anger, by the need to share my opinion, purely so that I could stand out or persuade someone of something. All those years wasted on attempting to explain myself, to feel less alone, to find allies. But now I felt full and warm, as if I were fetus in the maternal womb, as if I were floating in broth. Maybe my cells were alkalinizing, or maybe the genes of a new species of reptile were engulfing my human chromosomes. It wasn't such a bad feeling, this absence of empathy.

I went back home on foot, just as I had done on the way there. My legs felt tired, but I told myself that it was a good thing. Once again I crossed paths with people walking their dogs. It was time for the evening outing. I thought that this was why people got dogs in the first place. It was so that they had something on earth to cling to. To have a schedule, to leave the house, to have something to talk to other people about.

Easter Monday went by without any calls from Silvia. Usually we would always do something together on that day: a picnic at the park, a trip to the mountains to stuff ourselves with food and alcohol at a chalet or an inn while Silvia's less fashion-conscious friends—the ones she hung out with only on Easter Monday or during the summer—went on hikes. But that year I ended up spending it in front of the TV, watching biblical movies and thanking Jesus, our Lord and Savior, for having left us in such a cinematic manner. I also thanked the silence again for serving as my excuse. Without it, I would have been begging Silvia to take me with her, whatever her plans may be, like a dog does when its owner is preparing to leave the house.

The week passed and it was Friday again. Daniele usually turned up between a quarter past seven and half past seven. I stayed in bed until six twenty-five. Then, very lazily, I got out of bed, stripped off the bedsheets soiled from weeks of use, put them in the laundry basket, and put fresh ones out. It was too late for a bath, so I turned on the showerhead. My hair was so greasy that I had to shampoo it twice before I could actually feel my fingertips creaking against my scalp. I blasted a jet of cold water onto my face, shoulders, and the back of my neck, then stepped out. I trimmed my fingernails and rubbed moisturizer all over my body. I never normally did this, and the skin on my arms and my shins had begun to flake. The skin on my face also felt tight. It was as if I were desiccating. I returned to the bedroom and put on my best underwear, taking care for the first time in months—maybe years?—to match my underpants to my bra. In that moment, Daniele rang the doorbell. I wasn't dressed yet, and I was barefoot. I buzzed him into the building, then ran back to the bedroom. I stood there staring at the wardrobe. I couldn't choose. When I heard the front door bang shut, I closed the wardrobe. Daniele yelled a greeting and began looking for me. I'm here, I would have said. Sorry.

"Are you in the bathroom?" he asked. The confidence that had been in his voice earlier was gone now. "Oh, right. There you are."

He was wearing a dark blue suit. No tie, the first few buttons of his shirt undone. He looked very handsome.

My hair was dripping, I could feel the freezing water on my shoulders.

"It doesn't matter," he said. "I'll wait in the other room. I got us something to drink."

He said it very fast, as if to convince me that it truly didn't matter. I felt like I was torturing a kitten. He began to potter about in the kitchen; I could hear him opening and closing the cupboards, looking for glasses, opening the drawer where I kept the corkscrew. As he uncorked the bottle, I put on an Yves Saint Laurent dress from the winter 2008 collection, one of the last purchases I had made on Vestiaire. A gift to myself for the first three months of my silence.

Here I am, I would have said as I walked into the other room. I'm ready.

IT HAD BEEN months since I'd been to a restaurant, and seeing all those people shut away in the same room, all of them talking at the same time, caused me to lose my appetite. I kept breathing through my mouth and felt my lungs compressing as if the air outside my house were more rarefied. My shoes were uncomfortable, my dress was too big for me, and I kept having to check that it wasn't slipping off. I must have lost weight. I had bags under my eyes and my skin was dry and I was lavishly made up to cover it all, so that now I resembled a model who was addicted to drugs, one of those who look like their face might belong to an alien. Both of us must have seemed so strange—me, tiny and silent in my enormous dress, a caricature of a cover girl, and Daniele, who kept saying whatever came to his mind without expecting an answer, as if he were talking to someone on their deathbed, just to keep them company. Both of us dressed as if attending some grand gala. We were at one of those Japanese restaurants run by Chinese people, decorated exclusively in shades of black, white, and red so as to give the place as much of a Japanese vibe as possible. But the food was good. Daniele ordered for me, two *futomaki*, seafood udon, and mixed tempura. He almost got it right. We drank a bottle of Cartizze he had carefully selected from the menu, though I would have preferred an Asahi. I was drinking on an empty stomach, and the alcohol went straight into my bloodstream. I tried to maintain my composure. The humming all around us made it difficult for me to concentrate on what Daniele was saying.

When it was time for dessert, he ordered two green tea tiramisus and a bottle of sake. Then he said: “Let’s play a game.”

I emerged from my torpor and stared at him.

“The fact is, I still know very little about you, while I’ve told you almost everything there is to know about me. So I’ve been thinking, let’s try something: first I’ll recite all the things I know about you. Then I’ll start guessing.”

My eyes widened.

“Let’s pretend we’re on our first date. We’re getting to know each other. We’re trying to work out if this is going anywhere, even just sex for one night.”

I loved that he never used the word *fucking*, nor the hypocritical and outmoded *making love*.

“So. Your name is Cristina Martino, you’re twenty-eight, you’ll turn twenty-nine in May. You have an older sister and a nephew. You studied archaeology and ancient history, gradually losing interest in the limited job opportunities offered by your industry as well as in any other career opportunities, including in academia. You work at the faculty library on a fixed-term contract. Your salary lets you maintain a small but pleasant one-bedroom apartment on the river Dora, a scorpionfish, and a few material vices you very rarely indulge in as part of your rather frugal lifestyle, and most importantly, it allows you to set plenty of time aside for your greatest passion: silence. Since the beginning of the year, you have chosen to dedicate yourself to this fully and devotedly, sacrificing much in terms of leisure activities, interpersonal relationships, and equilibrium. An equilibrium that, all things considered, you have managed to keep, notwithstanding a little weight lost and a little less sleep. You have a birthmark on your right forearm, shaped like Corsica, and some lovely moles scattered all over your body, including a particularly memorable one on your left inner thigh. Sometimes you talk in your sleep. I don't know if it's something you've always done or if it began after you made silence your vocation, but either way, you do. Don't worry—none of it ever makes any sense. I think I once heard you say *saved. I'm saved*, I think it was. Maybe you were having a bad dream. But anyway, that's what you said before you rolled over. After that, nothing. You're very cute when you're asleep."

I swallowed what I had in my mouth with the last of the wine. I felt like I hadn't chewed at all and the food would come right back up if I didn't calm down.

"That's everything I know. It would be nice if it could be your turn now, but never mind. I'll just keep going. I don't know anything else about you—we didn't get enough time. But I can imagine a few things. Or make them up." He took a sip of sake and slowly swallowed it. "That tastes nice," he said, as if it even mattered. Around us, people were laughing and emitting a constant hum, a swarm of flies. I tried to concentrate on them but couldn't extrapolate anything that made any sense.

"When you were little, you talked a lot. You had an imaginary friend who was the only one who listened to you. You've always felt the burden of being compared to your sister, you don't even know when that started—it's a feeling that begins with your earliest memories. You've always felt that they listen to her more than they do to you, and when you were little you would scream and cry to draw attention to yourself. But you have always been very clever, and when you realized this was a childish thing to do, you stopped. Since then, you've never talked much; you didn't want to give them the satisfaction. You'd rather hold your words in than speak when you won't receive the appropriate attention. You hadn't realized until now, but you've been training for silence all your life. Keeping your judgments and opinions to yourself has never been a problem for you; people only share those for mutual gratification, or to hear someone tell them, one day, 'You were right all along' or to keep a conversation going. You've never been scared of boredom. You'd much rather not be seen as rude, and arrogance is among those human traits you least tolerate. But there's always a price to pay, right? You thought this would be appropriate. You care about people much more than you think. But you'll appeal to their goodwill. You've lost a few, and you will lose a few more. But you don't mind. You see it more as added value than collateral damage. A kind of sieve. People's goodwill is all you care about. You don't see this yet, but it's that misunderstood little girl who's talking now. At twenty-eight you can't shout anymore; these days if you want to be noticed, it's best to stay silent. That's not why you're doing this, but you don't mind it, either. No one will pass up a chance for revenge, not when it comes with the package."

I poured myself some sake. I held a sip of it in my mouth and swirled it against my palate until my teeth felt coated in that sweet, alcoholic patina.

"As for why you're doing this, that's a whole other story. You have many reasons, not just one, and revenge is not the main one. There is nobody you've shared all of those reasons with—you usually deploy one per person, or two or three at most. Or, I should say, you *deployed*. Purification: that's the reason you offered to people you were less intimate with. It's also the same word you used with those whose feelings you feared hurting. *Dissatisfaction, disgust*—these words you saved for those of a more rebellious nature. But the main reason is a feeling of inadequacy. You're twenty-eight years old but you feel like you've got another seventy-five weighing on you, and the world has slowly slipped from your grasp. It's not you the present day is speaking to. And even when it is, you don't understand what it's saying. So you respond with silence. Silence is your weapon. When you are silent, you are not judged. It's not dissatisfaction, and it's not disillusionment. You feel you don't have enough to offer. At a certain point, in a certain moment, you became convinced that whatever you had to say was *truly* not worth listening to. And that," he said, taking a sip of wine to restore his voice, "is a real shame."

He was done. He had let himself be carried in the flow and he hadn't even stopped to take a breath. He took one then, and his expression changed.

"Well," he said, touching my hand. "I've gone too far, haven't I? I'm sorry. I'm not used to talking to you, I didn't know how to stop. It's like in the movies when you see people talking to gravestones, letting out all the words they'd never said before, and you know it's just a movie because of that time you tried to do it yourself at your grandma's tomb and you couldn't get beyond hello. But I just kept going like I couldn't stop. I'm sorry, I didn't mean to hurt you."

I lowered my eyes. His expression was back to the one I knew, and it upset me more than the one I had just seen. I calmly stood up, taking the napkin from my knees and placing it onto the table, keeping every gesture under control so as not to draw attention. "Do you want to leave?" he said. He stood up, too, more noisily than I had, his movements now back to being clumsy and fearful. I thought he was going to remind me that we hadn't finished the sake, but he didn't. He insisted on paying for us both. "I'm the one who invited you," he said. I moved away and walked out before he was done.

"I'm sorry," he said once he'd emerged. I'd lit a cigarette and

I was standing with my back to him. My fur coat gave me some kind of comfort, so I kept my cheeks buried in it, only sticking my neck out to take another drag of smoke and blast it back into the air. "You're right," he continued. "I caused you pain by doing the very thing you are trying to break free of. You're right. We need to break free of it. I'll be silent. I'll do what you want. Just let me say this one last thing, though, OK? Afterward I'll stop. We'll be silent. I don't need words either—I've never needed them. Just let me say this, Cristina. I like you. I like you more and more and I'm willing to follow your lead, even to keep my mouth shut, if you want. I'll be by your side for as long as you need. But afterward, please say something. Anything. I miss your voice."

His hands were in his pockets, and I had the feeling that I was at least eight inches taller than him. He kept looking away, and whenever his eyes came back to me, they were the only thing in his body that still had some kind of volume. Everything else looked like it had shrunk in the wash.

A few more people left the restaurant, a group of four or five. They were laughing and being noisy. They lit their cigarettes, and a blond, heavily made-up girl with full lips and very long fingernails kept repeating the same sentence over and over. *Shame on you*, she was saying in English while the others all laughed. She was pointing at a guy as she did this, her imperfect pronunciation lengthening the first word and causing the digraph at the start of the phrase—which sounded more and more like a hiss with every iteration—to turn into a whistle.

I looked at Daniele. Our cigarettes were not yet finished. I blew out all the smoke I had in my lungs, took another drag, then expelled it again, until there was no oxygen left in there. Then I spoke.

"I don't want to see you anymore," I said, my voice faint.

May

WITHOUT THAT REGULAR Friday evening appointment, the weeks became infinite units of time. I slept less than ever before and my eyes hurt from all the hours I spent looking at screens, first at work and then at home, my back and my ass aching from endlessly browsing property, fashion, and antiques art websites while lying in bed semi-reclined. The sheets had needed changing weeks ago. On Saturdays and Sundays, when my parents or Elena came by to check that I was still alive, I kept the bedroom door closed and hoped they wouldn't take it upon themselves to go in there. From the moment they rang the doorbell, I had just over a minute to run to the bathroom, wash my face and brush my teeth, and tie my hair up. I had found a face moisturizer that worked miracles; it contained some kind of self-tanning serum that gave my skin a healthy glow without it looking like I was wearing makeup, which was the perfect way of covering up the greenish-gray tinge I would have otherwise revealed.

My father came less frequently, and occasionally skipped a week. My mother was always quick to justify his absences—he had plans with friends, he was unwell—but I knew they were all excuses. Whenever he came, he stayed silent too, and I knew that he would never have the courage to come on his own, because he would not know how to paper over the silence, and eventually the silence would have emptied him out. Neither my mother nor Elena had that problem, and this illustrates the only true reason why quiet and predominantly asocial people like to surround themselves with talkers: the latter are so adept at filling up voids that they make it a lot easier for the former to go unobserved. They would tell me about their weeks, Elena dividing her time between work, Elia, and a Lindy Hop class she had joined—with low expectations—at the urging of some other young mother she had met at her son's kindergarten, and my mother increasingly living the life of a retiree, faithfully keeping to her Tuesday and Thursday Pilates classes. Every Sunday she brought me Tupperware containers full of food—osso buco, quiches, pasta bakes—and took back the ones she'd brought the week before. "Did you eat it all?" she would ask. "You're so skinny. Don't you dare, now. Silence is one thing, fasting is quite another."

My mother had become accustomed to not receiving responses after marrying my father and, before that, through my grandmother, who was eighty-three years old now and whose attitude toward life had become as withered as the skin on the back of her hands. My mother would remark sometimes that fate had burdened her with other people's laconism, this baggage whose weight she must carry without ever knowing its contents; it was a bullet that had swerved around her and gone on to strike those in her life. It had started off with her mother, then gone on to hit her husband, and eventually it had reached me. I don't recall ever exchanging more than a few words with my grandmother, but I do remember some magnificent afternoons spent with her in front of the TV, back when I was a child, just us two, cradled by the words that issued from the screen but with the volume turned too low for us to be able to follow any of it, and thus with no meaning other than to make warm and welcoming the nothingness with which we had furnished the room. Distant, weightless voices, just like in the womb.

My mother always said whatever crossed her mind, tending to summarize, and asking questions to make sure we were still with her, while the rest of us, struck by the bullet of quietness, responded in sounds and monosyllables or else in some other precise yet cautious manner, but always betraying a degree of irritation, as if words were like thunderbolts that upended some kind of equilibrium. Her words, meanwhile, were like lint on a coat, which she brushed off with a quick flick of her hand that took them away from us as well, and made sure there was no trace left behind. Now that she couldn't do this anymore, she felt lost. Every time she came to see me, she disguised her defeat under the hardness of her expression and of the tone with which she addressed me—but I knew the truth, and I was consoled by the fact that silence was something that she knew well and that, in spite of everything else, tied her to her childhood.

Elena, who had not been touched by the bullet, was more pragmatic than my mother, though this wasn't always immediately obvious. But I knew this too, and I knew I could count on the irony with which, right from the start, she had slowly dismantled my campaign of silence. This was not just annoying but also very difficult to bear. She, more than anyone else, was really giving me a run for my money. More than my father could do with his sad eyes or my mother with her (failed) attempts to act as if nothing were happening. Every now and then I would burst out laughing and take refuge behind my hand, like a Victorian lady. Elena talked nonstop, but not in that rigid, slightly fearful way Daniele had, always checking how I was doing, as if I were a piece of steak cooking on the grill. She just talked, free and unhindered by the burden of having to wait for a reaction or some kind of judgment. With no questions to hold them back, her thoughts whirled around the room like a ballon whose knot has just been undone; there was no continuity across the topics she brought up, from work to the gym to Elia, who had stopped sleeping through the night, to Marco, who worried her because he wanted to quit his job. Every sentence sparked another, and on it went, a cycle without pause. I didn't think I had ever heard her talk so much. She'd even stopped apologizing. "I hope I'm not boring you," she'd said the first few times.

In fact, she didn't bore me. I didn't really listen to what she was saying, at least not always, but I did pay attention to the tone of her voice, to the pauses she took, to the frenetic way she caught her breath or took a sip of water or wine before starting again. In spite of all the words, the information, the detail, I sometimes became fixated on observing the movements of her mouth, the way her small teeth appeared under her upper lip, and reflected that I knew very little, almost nothing, about her. Her image was linked in my mind to the holidays we'd been on as children, and my earliest memories were tied up with those years when we still lived together and shared the same room, she in the top bunk and I in the bottom, the terrifying stories she would start to tell as soon as my mother turned the lights off, the lunches at our grandmother's when we would challenge each other to taste the pasta and declare whether or not it was cooked, the summertime swims, the makeup and the clothes I would surreptitiously borrow before putting them back, hoping she wouldn't notice.

Now she was a woman, another person, different in the way she moved and the words she chose, and who knew how long she had been like this. She talked and I watched her and it seemed to me that she was slowly getting rid of some kind of weight and returning to the Elena I knew, the Elena I had tried to be like, whose boobs I had envied when she hit puberty, making a mental note of which T-shirts and which bras showed them off most effectively—the kind of information I would be able to make use of once my own began to grow, if ever that day should arrive. This was still her, only a more confident version. She talked and seemed to become lighter, and I was glad to do her this favor, her voice transporting me back to a state of serenity I had once known, and by the time she left it was already dark and I would get into bed and manage to sleep through the night.

But the next day I would wake up in Sunday's cleansed and virgin light, and I would feel alone and ask myself why I was still doing this. If I had remembered to buy the necessary ingredients, I would make myself a toasted sandwich and wallow and bask in my bad mood until I thought of my sister again, of her relief at being able to speak so freely without being interrupted or judged, and so I would convince myself that this was the reason for the silence, to help others free themselves, and I would stare at the window and at the apartments on the other side of the glass, trying to forget how much other people irritated me whenever I had no choice but to talk to them.

When they ran out of topics, Elena and my mother started to worry. They would peer at me as if to spot the more obvious signs of instability, before pleading with me to do something, to see someone, to get help. "You're wasting away," my mother would say. "Your father is very worried about you." Sometimes she got angry, then calmed down again and sat on the sofa. I would sit next to her and she would tuck my hair behind my ear, and that would be the best moment of the whole week.

"Your father also went through a tough time after they found that tumor. He started seeing a psychologist, who really helped him deal with the fear and get back on track after the surgery. He had become convinced that it was malignant and some part of his brain just wouldn't let go. This person really helped him out. Then you girls gave us Murphy, and that silly little boy did the rest. Here, look, I've written his name and phone number down. You can go and see him, even if you don't want to tell him anything. Just having someone qualified looking after you might be enough to make you feel better," she said.

Elena also kept saying the same kind of thing. "Why don't you get some help?" That was one of the most depressing euphemisms for therapy that I could think of. One day she turned up with a flyer. The image was of a wooden walkway over water—a lake, perhaps—and the text, printed in an indigo hue that echoed the same bland color scheme of the image, said, *Self-Help Group*. Below that, *Selective Mutism*. I looked at my sister and felt like my face was on fire. I felt betrayed. The fact that there should be a name for what I was doing seemed like an affront; if it had a name, then I wasn't alone, and if I wasn't alone, then what was the purpose of this? Elena turned the flyer over in my hands so that I would read the back.

Selective mutism is a childhood disorder that manifests in an inability to speak in social contexts such as school or in front of other people. But we often forget that SM can also persist into adulthood. As such, it is a condition that can cause difficulties in scholastic and work environments and lead to social isolation and relationship difficulties. Like children, adults with SM are overwhelmed with extreme anxiety and a petrifying fear. Mutism can also be a manifestation of post-traumatic stress disorder, developing in the wake of exposure to a traumatic experience.

Had I still possessed my voice, I would have pointed out that none of this had anything to do with me. I might even had added, *You know nothing about me*, and we would have ended up fighting. But with no response to give, I felt much less annoyed. I was sorry to see her and my mother so distressed. I would have told them that the solution was silence. That they should also give it a go. I, for example, had discovered that it was the one thing in the world that I did best.

I SPENT MY birthday in bed. It was a Wednesday, and I had taken the day off. People at work had begun to suspect that the whole throat-illness story was a lie, and they kept trying to corner me with improvised and pitying monologues in which they sought to ascertain the state of my mental health. Ever since I had stopped talking, Patrizia had taken a maternal attitude toward me, and kept saying things like "Don't worry, I know you can't respond" or "If there's anything you haven't understood, just write it down for me on a piece of paper." But during the last few days her manner had become more brusque, if not even abrupt; she was less indulgent toward any mistakes I made, and more impatient. I was flattered. She was the person who made me feel most proud and capable: when she spoke to me, I gave nothing back. A total absence of facial expressions, an introverted look, nothing for kinesics experts to analyze. Aponia and ataraxia. I was a plant, a stone, a utensil. I was Harpo. I could have been Harpo. I found that everything was easier with her. The more impassive I remained, the more it irritated her. And the more irritated she was, the more invisible I became. That and the pittance that was credited to my account every month were the only reasons I bothered to wake up in the morning, get out of bed, slather my miracle cream onto my face, and walk out into the world.

But today was my birthday, and I was going to honor the occasion. I was twenty-nine years old and I hadn't had a conversation in nearly four months. We were well into spring and everything out there had woken up; my apartment infested with light and by the songs of stupid birds exchanging mysterious messages of death and life. Their affected chirping was interrupted by the sound of crows, whose cawing was as primitive and ungraceful as the way they trotted along the ground. I took my phone out of the top drawer in the wardrobe and switched it on. It had been off for several days. In March my parents had gifted me a telephone and a landline account: they and Elena were the only ones who had the number, and every now and then they would call me on it to check that I was there and to talk about themselves. Other than that, I only used my mobile phone to send text messages to Patrizia informing her of an absence or a delay.

My mother sent me messages on WhatsApp, which she already knew I would not reply to. She would tell me how her day had been and end with "How's everything with you?" That day, she and Elena had both sent me voice notes. The message from my parents had been sent at seven twenty-five in the morning—my mother reminding me of the precise moment of my birth, my father interjecting to say, "Mummy's made you chocolate cake." Elena's message had come half an hour later; she'd sent it from her car, probably while dropping Elia off at preschool. "Wish your aunt a happy birthday," she said imperiously. Then the voice note cut out and was immediately followed by another. "Sorry," this one said, "some idiot just ran a red light. See you tomorrow night?" I remembered that they had tried to invite me round for dinner on my birthday itself, but I had pretended that I was busy.

With my phone before me and WhatsApp now open, I started going through older messages. Among those that remained unread, there were none from Silvia and one—a single, extremely lengthy one—from Daniele, dated April 21. I responded to my family with a random emoji, turned my phone off, and lowered the blinds. I ordered noodles the way I used to back when I was going out with Giacomo, then drank a bottle of gewürztraminer. For the hundredth time, I watched *Indiana Jones and the Temple of Doom*, which was my favorite. Then I watched *Raiders of the Lost Ark* and *The Last Crusade*, before ordering pizza and watching *Jurassic Park*. I knew all the dialogue off by heart, and it was relaxing to let myself be lulled by familiar words, with nothing that could surprise or unsettle me.

My bed was full of crumbs and my mind was clouded by alcohol. I downed my first glass of water of the day, fed Harpo, and switched my phone back on, keeping it on airplane mode. I tried listening to the voice notes Giacomo had sent me back in the day, but without backups, time had erased them. The TV was showing infomercials for improbable gadgets, which made me think back to that time when slimming shorts were all the rage, as well as those electrodes that were supposed to be as effective as going to the gym. I thought of Giacomo again and tried to remind myself of what his voice sounded like, but I couldn't. I tried resurfacing the traces of past conversations, but it was as if they had been submerged in layers and layers of soil and sand. Maybe during the time when we were together we had developed some kind of silent language, like some elderly couples do.

Maybe that was what had happened and I'd realized it only now. I picked up my phone again. Giacomo's voice notes had been erased, but Silvia's hadn't. I again listened to her voice from last year's chats. I listened to her making plans for the weekend, griping about some clerk in a government office or about losing her house keys, insulting some mutual acquaintance who had put up yet another bullshit post on social media, celebrating her latest purchase, imploring me to snip her tubes and have her disbarred after a terrible date with some guy who kept a framed photo of his mother on his bedside table and who, at the peak of their sexual encounter, had asked Silvia to suck her thumb. I listened to all of this until I had the feeling that I could reply to her, say something useful: a joke to make her laugh, a sentence that would have wound back time.

I had no voice notes from Daniele with which to torment myself. Only a series of polite messages and a letter he had sent me the week before, and that I did not wish to reread because it frightened me. But I didn't have his voice. *I miss you*, I would have told him if I'd had a voice note to cling to. I longed for his words, uttered seemingly without effort but fully aware of his interlocutor's immense and silent effort. Spreading into the air around us like incense covering the scent of a corpse. I missed his empty chatter, the small talk and basic one-way conversations. That is what I would have told him, and I would have thanked him for never having asked for anything in return. I would have also told him a quote from Novalis that I had noted down months before and that kept circling in my mind. I would have told him that whenever someone speaks just for the sake of speaking, they will come out with the most splendid, original truths.

The next day, then, I had no choice but to go to my parents' place for dinner. My mother's chocolate cake had been decorated with white writing that looked like it was made of plastic, and said *Happy Birthday Cristina*, as if I were turning six. Elena, Marco, and Elia had also come, and my parents looked so happy to have me there that I went as far as to blow the candle out for their enjoyment. The air that came out of my mouth was silent, and I presented it to them in exchange for their affection. We cut the cake and I watched my name, spelled out in chocolate, break into pieces to be swallowed up and ground into mush by their teeth, which seemed to me like an appropriate end for it. It was a good gift, and I was grateful for it.

I started going to the self-help group from Elena's flyer, just to have something to think about other than myself. The group met every Thursday evening in a Gestalt therapy center. There were four other people there, and I was the oldest one. I knew this because of the form that was given to us at the first meeting, which, alongside a few pages of information with headings like *What is selective mutism?* and *What is acquired mutism?*, also contained data about the various participants: names and surnames, dates of birth, and email addresses—all this, I imagined, in the vain hope that people might feel the urge to contact one another. Two of the participants were teenagers, one was twenty-one, and the youngest was a ten-year-old girl accompanied by her mother, who sat in an antechamber outside the meeting room and waited for the hour to pass, watching videos on her phone with the volume turned up high.

In the room with us, we had a moderator. She was in her thirties and had gone through a mute phase herself in the past. She was called Sara, a name composed of two fairly similar syllables that were easy to pronounce. Sara's job was essentially to speak in our stead, and thus avoid these meetings turning into a circle of silence. According to the theory that if we want to make people feel comfortable and convince them to reveal their secrets, we must first give them something of our own to chew on, Sara talked to us about how she had refused, for three years, not only to speak a word but even to leave her room. She had received some help from an association of *hikikomori*, whose behavior was similar to hers—though they were mostly men. She told us this with a tinge of pride in her voice, as if being the only woman in that community had been a small triumph. She said that it all began when, aged sixteen, she had refused to go to school because she was fed up with spending her days curled up in a corner while all the other girls her age *blossomed* around her. She had felt too different from them, and so she had concluded that it would be better to shut herself up in her room.

She had already suffered from selective mutism in primary school, she added. She had recovered slowly from that, managing at first to communicate with small groups of people, and eventually extending her range until she had been able to make new friends. She'd almost managed to lead a normal life in middle school, but in high school she had "plunged once again into mutism and isolation—at precisely the time when most people would expect a young woman to start wanting to go out, to go dancing, to become interested in the opposite sex, to have her first experiences of romance." When she spoke, her words sounded like something you would read in a printed book, and I figured it must be due to all that abstinence. I wondered if the same thing would happen to me, should I ever decide to go back. Had I possessed my voice, I would have told her that all of this was counterproductive and that she was scaring me.

She explained to us that selective mutism in adults was somewhat rare. "Sometimes, as in my case, it can be a recurrence of mutism experienced during the developmental stage. In certain cases it can derive from a particular form of social anxiety, and in others it is a consequence of trauma. These are all disparate causes, and they are not really comparable. But we are not here to deal with causes. There is psychological support available for that, and I am sure many of you are already availing yourselves of it. And if you are not yet doing so, I would remind you that the center which is currently hosting us is full of people who would be willing to meet with you. But as I was saying, we are here this evening for a different reason. We are here to share a state of mind. Though it may originate in different places, the end result is the same: we are not able to communicate. This, then, is a safe space where you will not be asked any questions but where—even in silence—you can be close to people who understand how you feel, know what you are going through, and share the same thoughts and preoccupations as you do."

At this point she got up and took from a table next to the wall some A4 notepads and felt-tip pens, handing them out to us and asking us to use them to answer some questions. "But also to communicate whatever you may wish to communicate," she said. "Usually," she continued, "in groups like this we would start with introductions. But our group is a little different, isn't it? I would therefore suggest that we skip that formality. Instead I will ask you to draw a picture. It doesn't matter if you're not good at it—this is not an art class. The reason we are here is to not be judged and to not judge in turn, and it's important that this should be clear right from the outset. We all struggle with judgment, right? We are among equals here."

She stopped and took a sip from the bottle she was holding. She must have drunk at least half of it already, since we'd started. I wondered how she was going to hold on for an hour without needing the toilet, and I saw that she had another bottle, as yet untouched, on the floor under her chair.

"On that piece of paper," she resumed, "I would like you to draw something. I would like you to choose an image that will describe how you are feeling in this moment. It could be anything; let your imagination run free. And it doesn't necessarily have to be an object or some concrete thing either. Again, if you don't know how to draw, don't worry about it. Once everyone has finished—and I'll be participating too—we will show one other what we have produced. I will not attempt to comment on your work, nor seek to decipher the sensation that might have generated it. We will show one another our pictures, and that will be it; they will act as our visiting cards. Like those sticky labels with people's names on them that you see at Alcoholics Anonymous, you know?" she said, giggling in a rather nervous manner. She opened her bottle again and took a sip. "It could be as simple as a drawing of the sun, a cloud—it's all fine. Something of you. It doesn't matter what, and it doesn't matter how much."

She gestured with her hand as if to say "Begin" and went back to drinking. Then, as if she'd forgotten to do so before, she looked at the clock and told us: "I'll alert you when it has been ten minutes. We'll take ten minutes." Keeping to her promise, she put the bottle next to the second bottle under her chair, opened the notebook she had placed on her lap, pulled out the felt-tip pen tucked into the spiral binding, and began to draw.

I looked around. One guy had his head bent over his sheet but had made no move to use the felt-tip pen. I thought he must be the twenty-one-year-old: he had long hair, tied back, and a bristly, patchy beard like a meadow scorched by the sun. He looked like someone who hadn't showered in ages. The little girl kept doing what she'd been doing ever since she had arrived: scribbling on a sheet of paper, now using the notepad. But at a certain point she turned over onto the next page and began to put pen to paper with greater care. The other two, a boy and a girl—he was tall and large, with glasses and hair cut very short, while she was very skinny, with dark, protruding eyes that seemed to spread all the way to her cheeks—were looking away. Our gazes never met. I watched surreptitiously as they stared into nothing until they eventually gave in and started drawing something, too. I was the last one left.

I picked up the pen, took off the cap, and sniffed. In middle school, I had discovered with my best friend at the time—her name was Laura, though I suppose it still is Laura; it's just that we are no longer friends—that sniffing the tips of whiteboard markers gave us a high, so we would steal them and put them in our pencil cases without their caps on, and when the teacher was busy teaching, we would lean over and inhale the smell. I couldn't think of anything else now: just the markers that made classes more fun and Sara, our moderator, who drank compulsively between one word and the next and spoke in the mechanical tone of artificial intelligence. Now that she was drawing, she looked kind of whole again. But when she spoke, I feared—between one pause and the next—that she was going to break, disintegrating into a thousand little squares, like in *Cube*. It's the same anxiety I feel every time I go to the theater, which is why I hate going to the theater. What happens if an actor forgets a line? What happens if they forget *all their lines*? It's a feeling I cannot tolerate. It feels to me like spectating at a public execution, except for some reason the moment keeps getting delayed. It's worse than standing on the edge of a cliff. I don't know how people do it.

Drawing: Did I still remember how? I hadn't tried in years. I remembered the little white-and-yellow desk that had previously belonged to Elena, where I used to sit and color things for hours, at first just with felt-tip pens and later with watercolors, too. It was as good an excuse as any to disappear from reality, to be told "Well done" and be left undisturbed. *What are you doing? I'm drawing. Don't distract me.* When they asked me what I wanted to be when I grew up, I told them I wanted to be a postal worker. I was fascinated by these uniformed people who traversed many kilometers to deliver messages that weren't theirs. I imagined them as people with no life of their own, devoted, enslaved, taking vows of celibacy as if they were priests or nuns. I drew a crucifix in the handful of minutes we had left, putting every effort into it.

When Sara said we were out of time, everyone lifted their felt-tip pens from the paper and sat staring at what they had produced. They were very obedient. I had a feeling that as small children they must have been their parents' pride and joy—at least until they had turned into a cause for concern. Years spent wondering where they had gone wrong. If I could have responded, I would have told them that their only mistake had been to force their children to step out into the world.

Sara asked us to take turns showing our drawings. "I'll start," she said. "To break the ice." She lifted her piece of paper. "As you can see, I'm not the best. I hope you can figure out what it's meant to be."

There was a mirror taking up half the page, with undulations designed to simulate a reflective surface. In front of the mirror, a stylized little man. The lines of the drawing were pretty confident and crisp. Was our Sara hiding some kind of artistic talent? In any event, I appreciated the effort. It felt necessary.

"Right. I've always been very shy. The thing that scared me most was people's judgment, and so I thought: If I don't speak, nobody can make fun of me for what I say, right? This went on for years before I understood—and I mean really understood—that I was the only one judging me. People do not form their opinions on the basis of a single action; it's more like a sum total. But we will have lots of time for that," she giggled. She was embarrassed, and I felt embarrassed for her.

"Right," she repeated. "I'm talking too much. Now it's your turn. Who wants to show us their drawing? Let it speak for you. You won't need to do anything except show us."

This drew a blank, as might have been expected. I wasn't sure Sara knew what she was doing, but I was sure that in that moment, everyone else hated her. The anger was palpable. How could she not feel it? How could she not succumb to it? I increasingly suspected that it was all a bluff. It was a paradoxical situation: a support group in which nobody shares their story, and without the bit where you go, "Hello, my name is X and I'm an alcoholic." It seemed to me that in this version, everybody could be the same as everybody else. It would have been easier if they hadn't given us those sheets at the start, if they hadn't given each of us a name. Placed in that room without an identity, without a past, we would be the closest thing to the doctrine of Christ since the time of Christ. We ought to have all started wearing the same clothes: neutral, boring colors, natural fibers, unremarkable designs. A cult with a single unifying precept, proving right all those who kept analyzing the choice I had made as if it had been their own.

But all of a sudden, the little girl, the youngest of us all, lifted her piece of paper and showed it to the room. It was all over. We were about to name ourselves. With the still-uncertain hand that belied her age, but admittedly also with a certain amount of talent, she had drawn a heart of ice. The heart was not heavily stylized but looked more like something out of a comic book: veins and arteries entered into the atria and ventricles; the aorta grasped the pulmonary artery. Icicles hung in the hollows of the veins. She showed us her drawing for a few seconds, then placed it back on her lap, its blank back facing upward. She lowered her head as if she were expecting Sara to comment, to judge. We all did. But all Sara said was "Thanks," before asking if anyone else wanted to show their work. She said *work* as if we were paid professionals. No one was brave enough to step up, so she took over: "Let's go clockwise, then. Giovanni, would you like to show us your *work*?"

According to the dates of birth listed on the forms we had been given, Giovanni must have been seventeen, but he looked at least ten years older. He was submerged in his chair. His hands, small and puffy like a newborn's, clung to the piece of paper, which rustled in the funereal silence. With his elbows tucked into his thighs and his torso bent forward, he looked like an amateur sculptor's attempt at tackling the theme of *inadequacy*. This posture was his way of securing room for himself in that space, a space that was essentially forcing him to be present, to show himself; and so, without even realizing what he was doing, he curled up like a dog, hoping to endear himself to people and not be told off. Nonverbal language, I thought, is only deceptive for those who don't listen to it. For those who deem it to be inferior to words and don't show it enough regard. You only start to understand it when there is no alternative.

Giovanni steeled himself and showed us his sheet. No drawing, only a few sentences written in extremely conscientious handwriting—feminine, one might say. They read: *I can't draw anything. Sorry. I'm happy to meet you all.* I thought: There goes the first victim.

"No problem, Giovanni. As I said, it doesn't matter if you can't draw very well—just a rough sketch like mine is perfectly fine," Sara said, giggling again. "But it's also fine not to draw anything at all. It is important that you do not see anything that happens in here as being an obligation. Rather, it should feel like a possibility. One to seize, if you feel up to it; otherwise perhaps it'll be for next time. The relationship we are trying to build here is one based on trust, and there will never be any impositions or ultimatums. The brief thoughts you wrote down are already a lot to go on. Thank you for sharing them with us. And we, too, are happy to meet you. I'm sure I speak for everyone here when I say so."

She paused, then said: "Elena, it's your turn."

The girl was sixteen and had the same name as my sister. She flipped her piece of paper over quickly, as if to shrug off the weight of that chore and return to her comfortable state of oblivion. Her eyes were so wide open they looked like they might pop out of her face. Her drawing was of a wolf in front of a gigantic full moon. The wolf's jaw was clenched shut and its head was not—as in the more traditional iconography—raised toward the sky, but lowered. It was a basic, nervous sketch, but we all stared at it for as long as she allowed us to. There was something curious about it. The wolf looked sad, but I kept thinking of it howling in secret, to avoid drawing the herd's attention, the deep howl fixed somewhere inside the belly or the head. The subject matter was banal, but if there had been some kind of prize at stake for this idiotic competition, Elena would have won it.

"We can all hear this drawing speak to us, right?" said

Sara, destroying the spell. "Thank you, Elena. Your turn now, Cristina."

It was my turn. I flipped my piece of paper around and showed everyone my stupid cross. I had shared something that was not necessary. Something even less necessary than the words I had growled at Daniele. With that cross, I once again renounced my nameless and aimless divinity, and relinquished silence.

"Thank you" was all Sara said. "Tommaso, you're the last one left. Would you like to show us your drawing?"

Tommaso did not move. He stared at Sara, his mouth half-contorted into a grin, just a trace of it, too lopsided to be considered a smile. He shook his head no. A pause, then another shake of the head.

"No?" said Sara. She waited a moment, but Tommaso stuck to his grin.

"All right," said Sara. Her tone was outraged, but she tried to hide it. "No problem. You'll do so when you feel ready," she said, and took a sip of water.

She looked at her watch. "Our first hour together is over. It was a pleasure to meet you, and to discover something about you all. Your silence is something about you. It is a starting point, and it is something we share. Something we love and that causes us pain at the same time. We will work to give it the space that it is due, not to chase it away but to prevent it from possessing us and our lives. To make sure that we are the ones controlling it, not the other way round. We will take our time to get there. Time is on our side. We are in no rush."

She stood up suddenly before concluding: "See you next week. Thank you very much."

She left quickly, taking her empty water bottle and leaving us on our own. Some of the others were already standing and followed her out. I calmly gathered my things and waited until I could be the last one to leave.

Outside it was dark and I would need to take the bus home. I went to the bus stop to wait, alone, surrounded by the bluish hue of the already greatly lengthened days and the fresh, cloying smell of spring in the air, as ruthless as it was every year.

Still May

I SLEPT VERY LITTLE. I couldn't stop thinking about that guy. The way he had rejected the exercise, so spontaneously and decisively, was proof that I still had work to do. How long does it take to become totally free? Perhaps I wasn't purifying myself enough. If only there were a lever I could pull that would flush out all the residue of my previous life in one go, like astronauts dumping their excrement into space. Giacomo told me once that he thought I worried too much about doing the right thing. No shit. "I really don't care what other people think," I replied. He said, "I think you do. You have a problem child complex." I looked it up online but couldn't find any condition bearing that name.

I got up, made breakfast, switched on the TV. It was nine o'clock and I didn't have to be at the library until two in the afternoon. The normal channels were broadcasting morning talk shows and cartoons for kids at home with fever. The Hanna-Barbera ones were still popular. I fed Harpo while the voices of *The Flintstones* played in the background. It was my favorite cartoon. I watched as Harpo plucked his feed from the surface of the water with little open-mouthed nibbles, lightning fast, to avoid breathing in too much air. Same as if we had to fish noodles right out of a bowl of soup, plunging our mouths and noses into the broth at the risk of drowning.

Once Harpo had finished with his feed, I picked up a defrosted shrimp and offered it to him, holding it between my fingers. I dunked it in the water and pulled it out again, calling Harpo to me as if he were a dog. He came closer and I waited like that, with the shrimp suspended just above the surface of the water, until he performed the action I had hoped to witness ever since the day I'd brought him home: this little piranha disguised as a porcupine made a tiny leap—with a flutter, or so it seemed to me, of the microscopic muscles under his spines—and plucked the shrimp from between my fingers before diving back into the water. He had decided to trust me. "Good fish," I told him. My voice was hoarse and dry, and if I'd recorded it and played it back, it would have scared me. I started coughing. I made myself an herbal tea with honey and drank it by the window, spying on all the people who had things to do.

The one thing I missed, sometimes, were hugs. I could feel the need for some kind of physical contact that might exempt me, however fleetingly, from having only myself to deal with, from having to endure my body on my own. Some nights I dreamt that Harpo was big and soft and that I could bring him into bed with me. Sometimes I dreamt he was a bear. You can tell nature's a bitch by looking at bears: deadly creatures with soft bellies and cute little ears you could just eat up. I wonder if sweetness only works on humans. With animals, nature is more direct: if a flower or a reptile is vivid in color, it has to be some kind of trick. Animals know and fear this, while humans are attracted to it. Nature had crafted Harpo not like a bear but like the *Amanita muscaria*. White polka dots on a red background are so improbable that clearly they must signal some kind of danger. Every scale on Harpo's body evoked the need for distance, yet I would have loved to squeeze him to me. "Do you love me?" I would ask him in my thoughts as I fed him, as I watched him breathlessly devouring his shrimp. It was the one sentence I regularly felt the need to utter, and that I still had to fight the urge to say out loud.

The truth was that no matter how much I tried, I would never be like that guy from the support group. I would always worry about coming across as disrespectful, rude, disappointing. I would always envy people who weren't like me, and I would always have to resist the temptation to run after those who were no longer there. Every time I heard a song that reminded me of Silvia, I would feel a sting in my throat; every time I heard something about a mutual acquaintance, such as an old classmate we both hated—the kind of thing I would have once seen on Facebook but that was relayed to me these days by my mother or my sister during their endless weekend monologues—every time this happened I would be tempted to break the silence and give Silvia a call. I would think of Giacomo watching a film we had already seen together, and the words I would have liked to say to him would feel like dead fish in my throat. I would think about Daniele, his questions, which required no response, and the mercy he was capable of, about everything I would have liked to give him in return but I never would, not because I was inconsiderate or inept but because I was mean, quite simply mean, and like all mean people, I went after the weak. I hated people because they did not understand me, and when they did, I hated them even more. Renunciations were no use. They wouldn't make a dent in my soul.

But that guy, that Tommaso, it was as if he'd been carved

from stone. The way he'd shaken his head, with no fear or shame, showed he was a more faithful devotee than I—for I was sure he *must* have dedicated himself to silence, too. I felt the urge to call the center that hosted us on Thursdays to ask them for his phone number or his address, so that I could go over there and beg him to be my guide. *Guide me*, I would say to him, though without ever breaking the silence. I pictured him as some kind of modern-day holy man, like the ones who deliver sermons on social media, who had suddenly decided to stop. I saw him as a compelling presence, one of those rare people with charisma who choose not to take advantage of this mysterious and unevenly distributed talent, and instead embrace defeat, opting for the path of misery and marginalization, no cult and no followers, only the sound their thoughts make inside their heads every day.

I sent Patrizia an email saying I felt unwell and would not make it to work. *I need to see a doctor's note*, she replied. I googled *how to get doctor's note for work*: apparently I had to ask my family doctor. I'd had the same family doctor since I was fourteen, and he also knew my parents well. He liked me. I'd had a checkup shortly after the start of the silence. "You seem a little debilitated," he'd remarked. "Your mother told me what's been going on. You know there's no shame in admitting when something's not right." I'd made a face at him and grabbed a fruit gummy from the bowl on his desk, just as I used to do when I was a teenager and went to see him to have my lungs checked after a bout of bronchitis. He had written me a prescription for food supplements and given me the name of a psychologist he recommended. Now here I was again, sending him an email. *I have a temperature, I need a note for work*, I wrote. *You'll have to come in*, he replied. *Are you able to do so?* I thought, This doesn't make sense. *It's only a mild one, but it might get worse if I go out. Can't you just email me the note?* I waited several minutes for his response, constantly refreshing the page. Then I wrote again: *I'm taking the food supplements. I'm getting help.* It was a half-truth. After a while, he replied: *Well done. Take care of yourself.* He'd attached the note.

DANIELE LIVED OUTSIDE the city. According to Google, the quickest way to get there was to take a train followed by a bus. I decided to take the train and walk the rest of the way. It was lunchtime, and the car was full of kids on their way home from school. I still recalled those days with horror, waking up at a painful six a.m. when it was still dark outside. When I started secondary school, we still lived outside Turin, in a town with a population of five thousand and a high school that was only six kilometers away but that I couldn't attend because my mother taught there. I suppose I could have enrolled in another teacher's class, but even so I would have still been "Malagoli's daughter," and that would definitely have not been fun. My sister had barely survived it all.

I decided to attend a high school in the city, where I could blend in with the other pupils, just one among many. At the end of the school day I would take the bus in the opposite direction and be home at around half past two, lunching on what my mother and sister had left for me before shutting myself in my room to watch MTV or afternoon TV shows until four o'clock. I would do a little bit of homework too, just to ease my conscience, and go out with the two or three friends I still had left from primary and middle school, who attended my mother's high school and had begun to bore me a little because of their obsession with trendy sneakers, their straightened hair, and their platonic devotion to senior-year student council reps, which they manifested by drawing little hearts in their school diaries.

This had all gone on until we moved to Santa Rita the year after. A neighborhood that struck me as aesthetically repulsive—its buildings, designed in the sixties and seventies for Turin's factory workers, erected side by side with no breathing room, and a church in the style of the Romanesque revival which bore no relation to its surroundings, except for a bell tower almost as tall as the surrounding blocks—but at least it was in the city. I gradually replaced my friends from primary and middle school, just as they were doing with me. Silvia joined our class in the third year of high school, having failed her end-of-year exams the year before. We would often go over to her place after school: she lived in a nicer neighborhood, in a bigger house that—most importantly—was always empty, as her parents worked late hours. After lunch we would turn on the TV and smoke weed or hashish, depending on what we had been able to source.

We got our supplies once a week from an old classmate of hers who lived behind Piazza Vittorio. He lived alone in an enormous house that was very old and sparsely furnished and had been left to him and his older brother by their parents, though we had never understood whether they had died or simply moved back to their native country. We'd go there and smoke all together, huddling under smelly blankets, due to the boiler often being broken. The record player was always on and only ever stopped running when the record came to an end, at which point anyone who could be bothered to would get off the sofa and pick the next album from a vast collection. That was when Silvia started calling me Martinez, after she spotted Boss Hog's *Whiteout* and declared that Cristina Martinez was my punk blues alter ego.

Cristina Martinez actually looked more like Silvia than me, though at the time both of us wore our hair very long, and kept it straight and dark. But while Silvia had a model's physique and the fierce expression and perfectly shaped mouth that would very soon enable her to start making enough money for university and everything else, I still bore the rounded features of adolescence, and they seemed to have no intention of going anywhere. My giant cheeks and high cheekbones traded punches with my nose, which—unlike my breasts—had suddenly begun to grow until it looked identical to my father's, with wide nostrils and a rounded tip. Silvia's lips were full and very red, even without makeup; mine were thin, my mouth so wide that only my dentist was happy with it, with small, untidy teeth that I tried my best to hide by making sure I never smiled in photographs. In any case, the assonance between our names was amusing. So from that day onward, or pretty soon thereafter, Silvia began to call me Martinez, and I started using black eye shadow and wearing lipstick on Friday and Saturday evenings, when we would settle in for a predinner drink in one of the bars in Piazza Vittorio or along the river. All of this made our one-year age gap feel less obvious to me. I would often joke that we were such a cliché: the outgoing, popular girl paired with her more reserved classmate, the *cool girl* and her melancholy, somewhat nondescript sidekick who lets herself be dragged into a world of sin. Silvia would tell me to cut the bullshit.

"You're the one all the boys are into," she'd say. "With me, they just want a quick spin. I'm too brash, I'm too much. They get bored of me eventually. But you, with that mysterious air of yours, *Hey, look at me, there's a whole world to discover*, you drive them crazy."

"Are you saying I'm a flirt? You hate flirts."

"Don't you?" she huffed. "Anyway, I'm saying the opposite, you idiot."

I stopped using heavy makeup many years ago, as I touch my face all the time and would just end up smudging my mascara all over my eye sockets and my eyeliner onto my cheeks, until I looked more like a boxer than a "bad girl." Besides, I felt old now. I had turned twenty-nine ten days ago, and these four months of silence seemed like the only good thing I had managed to do in my life so far. My relationship with silence was likely to become the longest one I'd ever had, and possibly the most faithful one, too.

"And you don't talk much," Silvia used to say. "Guys *love* the silent type."

"Not the kinds of guys I like."

The kids who were on the train with me that day made that journey daily and were ten or fifteen years younger than I was. When you're that young, my age seems very far away. I certainly didn't miss waking up at dawn, sitting at a classroom desk for five hours, listening to strangers talk at you. Though I was still doing that part now. I had taken our teachers' instructions to be quiet and listen so incredibly seriously that I'd nearly made a religion out of them. I felt like smiling, so I did, staring out the window at the maize just beginning to grow in the fields. I must have looked like an idiot. I hadn't smiled in months, or at least that's how I felt. I might have smiled a few times with Daniele. I imagined a young Daniele taking that train every morning and sitting down in class, saving up the things he wanted to tell his classmates until it was time for recess. His parents must have been very proud of him.

The train came to a halt two stops before mine. About thirty kids got off like a herd, and the car emptied. I turned the volume in my headphones up so as not to hear the voices of the ones that were still left; I didn't want their conversations to distract me from my thoughts. I tried to visualize the moment when I would be standing outside Daniele's house as if it were a memory of something I had already experienced. The short building, three floors, the shared front yard, the driveway, all of them just as I had observed on Google Maps. I'd found his address on an online phone book; I knew the name of the small town where he lived, and there was only one family with his surname.

His father, or the man I assumed must be his father, was a doctor. I could picture him from the stories Daniele had told me: a practical man, not particularly affectionate, devoted to his family but not as much as he was to his work. Demanding with his kids but kind to his wife, who followed a fairly conventional pattern by taking care of Daniele and his sister and supplying them with hugs and words of encouragement in lieu of their father's, too. She must have been a calm and affable woman, witty but controlled, and willing, in convivial settings, to sacrifice her own thoughts and opinions so as to avoid interrupting her husband's impassioned monologues. A family you might see in a drawing hanging on the wall of a kindergarten classroom, the product of any preschooler's imagination. My drawings were similar, except that my father was always in the corner, or at least smaller than me, my mother, and Elena. I'm sorry, Dad. I hadn't yet understood the value of the silence you were trying to teach me. I couldn't appreciate it. I'd seen a picture of Daniele's family in his photo gallery, that night I used his phone. His mother looked like a version of him but with a bob cut blow-dried by the local hairdresser. Holding her Tod's handbag close, an expensive Christmas gift from a particularly bountiful year. Daniele's father's hand was resting on his wife's shoulder. Daniele had an older sister who also looked like him, tall and confident, with lustrous, naturally copper-brown hair that she wore loose and wild; his friends would have called her a total hottie. Daniele didn't boast about her, didn't talk about her; it was a subject he tried to fend off with his customary polite smile. His sister had a traditional but memorable name, like Isabella or Ludovica, while Daniele had had to make do with his paternal grandfather's name. Daniele's father was from Puglia; his mother was Sicilian. But from Palermo, not Messina, like my own father. I was piecing together past conversations, from when I'd still responded, and the passionate monologues Daniele would deliver on our Friday evenings. Every piece had its place, and I tried to re-create the image of Daniele as if I were drawing up a psychological profile of a serial killer, all of it held together by my presumption that I knew everything. Giacomo would have said that I was good at working people out, though not as good as him. In the meantime, the countryside unfolded before my unseeing eyes, suggesting that I might wish to start getting ready.

Three boys and a middle-aged man got off at the same stop as me. I followed them to the exit and pulled out my phone so I could look at the map. I had to go straight for three hundred meters, turn right, then left, then right again. More than two kilometers in the Piedmont countryside, the fields still sopping wet with the May rains, though they would dry quickly enough. The air was already on its way to boiling, and the scent of summer was impossible to ignore. I tried to avoid major roads because I didn't know Daniele's schedule, and if he happened to be driving by just then, he would easily spot me on the side of the road. He would wonder who this madwoman was, walking along the edge of a fast-moving suburban highway, and why she was on foot rather than in a car or a bus or on a moped, like a normal person. He would slow down to avoid running the madwoman down, but also because she reminded him of someone he knew; he would have the feeling that he had seen the madwoman before, and once he got closer he would realize that he really did know her, and that she was indeed mad, so mad that, after months of silence, she had spoken for the first time to tell the only person who could still tolerate her to fuck off.

He would wonder what she was doing there, and perhaps he would even be a little scared. He would keep driving and he wouldn't go back home, not for a few more hours. No, if I walked on that road, I would ruin everything. Residential roads were better, the smaller ones where you could keep an eye on the oncoming cars and hide if need be.

As I walked, I peered through people's windows. You couldn't really see inside; the curtains left too much to the imagination, and I was sick of trying to imagine things. Once upon a time I might have tried to reconstruct other people's lives based on the clues they left behind—toys in the front yard or on the balcony, laundry hung up to dry, bicycles. Now it all seemed like a waste of time. Objects were objects, period. The more I stuck to facts, the less likely life was to take me by surprise.

Daniele's house was a three-story row house in a residential development made up of row houses. I recognized it from a distance; it looked just like the image I had seen on the maps app. It was nearly midday and the sun was beginning to burn; the hills all around had taken a yellowish hue in spite of the rains, so that they looked like enormous hunched-up stink bugs, biding their time, ready to swallow the whole village as soon as they woke up. I felt the fleeting impulse to warn Daniele, to beg him to get out of there and save himself, but then I remembered that

I hadn't come there to save him. *We are not responsible for other people's lives*, Giacomo had told me once.

I reached a patch of shade and caught my breath. I remembered that I had brought a bottle of water with me and thought this was the right moment to take it out of my bag. Now that I had reached my destination and could physically see Daniele's house, the attic with the round skylight he'd told me about, the perfectly manicured yard, the green fence, I wondered what I should do next. I had set out without a plan, and now that I was here, I felt as if I had been sleepwalking. My instinct was to look for a place to hide, as if I were being followed. The earth exuded heat, emitting a powerful apocrine smell. If I had been a dog, I would have gone crazy, sniffing at everything and barking at the sky. But I was not a dog. And I could not allow myself to be discovered.

I found the entrance to the cellar, or maybe it was where all the electric meters were stored, and went inside. A series of concrete steps led up to a heavy gray door. I stood there, storing up cold air; it must have been ten degrees cooler in there. What now? Would I buzz the intercom? Would I wait outside the front door, hoping to see him emerge? And what if he wasn't home alone, what if his parents or his sister were also there? "Mum, Dad, Rebecca, meet Cristina, my mute friend." After which he would politely kick me out, because turning up at his place with the hope that my presence alone might be enough to restore what little we'd had was probably the most self-important plan I'd ever come up with.

In that moment I realized that this was yet another of the many things I had done solely for my own sake, and that once again, this time unbeknownst to him, Daniele had bowed to my will. Merely being there, breathing in the same air, stepping out of the maps app's satellite view to observe with my own eyes the spaces in which he existed—all of it meant I could avoid thinking of him in terms of his absence, avoid being swallowed by nothingness. My lungs expanded, and it was no longer ninety degrees in the shade but seventy, with a spring breeze that felt like a promise, for the solar year begins neither in January nor in September but in March, while April bursts with possibilities, and May—if it is benevolent—makes them come true, except that May here is a wet month that rots the crops, so best to wait for summer, though one never learns anything useful from summer. I wasn't going to learn anything from this summer either, but at least I was able to take in some oxygen now and let some fresh air into my brain.

I would tell Daniele that I missed him, just like I missed so many things about life as it used to be, things that were now forever lost. And that if ever a gadget was invented to record the moments we experience in life and allow us to go back and watch them—so that there would be no need to rely on the mind's subjective evocation of the past, so that memories could become video files to be played back at will—then I would watch them again and again and make it my only hobby.

I would tell him that it wasn't him, it was me, and that it wasn't even me, it was the silence. I would tell him that between him and silence, I would always choose the latter, that I would choose silence over everything, really, because it was the spoonful of sugar for a medicine that would otherwise be impossible to take, a lifesaving medicine, and the more I distanced myself from things, the more I appreciated them. And I would have told him, *Let's please keep doing what we're doing, please, let's love each other from a distance without ever telling each other*, like Margot and Richie Tenenbaum, because it's the only way I know how.

I would tell him that I felt the same love toward everyone who had passed through my life then left because of me, that it was the most honest way of loving, the most honest way I knew of, and after all I wasn't asking for anything else, only to keep loving from afar, and I would be absolutely faithful and love him for the rest of my life, expecting nothing in return, because my life was full of love and I was fine. I would tell him not to worry, I was fine. I just missed our Fridays a little, only that, the films in bed and the words we told each other, but in truth this too was fine, because the words I spoke in my head were even better.

June

THE FOLLOWING THURSDAY EVENING, I went back to the therapy center. There was a new girl there who must have been twelve or thirteen, but she wasn't asked to do the drawing exercise. Sara welcomed her, told us the girl's name, cleared her throat, took a sip from her bottle, cleared her throat again, and started reading from a book I had never heard of before. I glanced at the cover and thought it must be one of those pseudo-psychology volumes where the author's own considerations are corroborated by a whole series of testimonials published under false names.

The passage she was reading concerned a boy who had lost both his parents in a car accident at the age of eleven. He had also been in the car, but he had survived with just a few scratches. When he was discharged from the hospital and entrusted to the care of his aunts and uncles, his family realized that he had stopped talking. They assumed at first that his mutism must be the result of some kind of physical trauma, a microlesion so tiny that all the tests had overlooked it, and so they subjected him to more specific examinations, but still nothing emerged.

Having thus excluded any organic sources, they'd had to

resign themselves to the fact that the trauma they'd been looking for must be emotional. The child had stopped communicating altogether: he did not emit any sounds, he didn't write, didn't draw, didn't use gestures. When he wasn't asleep, he just sat there with his eyes wide open and staring into space. If someone tried to force him to talk, asking too many probing questions, or if a stranger got too close, watched him too carefully, or even just touched him, the boy would freeze, like prey playing dead. When he was at home, he was able to get on with his life almost normally, doing everything he used to do before: he played, watched TV, had afternoon snacks, and—reluctantly—ate some vegetables too, like any kid his age. But at school he would freeze. He would spend whole mornings sitting completely still, staring at the teachers or at the blank notebook before him, fiddling with his pencil instead of using it to fill in the multiple-choice tests his grammar teacher went out of her way to design specifically for him—at first with four possible answers for each question, then only two, but even that made no difference. The only homework he would do was for his math class: algebraic equations were his way of opening up to the world, his only means of communication, the only kind of response he would ever give.

Middle school algebra. Geometry. I remembered that grandiose feeling, that intoxicating sensation of purity I used to get whenever I solved a problem correctly, the reassurance in knowing that there was an incontrovertibly right answer and an infinite series of possible ways to go wrong, but as long as you followed all the procedures carefully, as long as you made an effort to do everything properly, you would arrive at the truth. A truth nobody could deny, because numbers are tangible and real, nothing at all like words. I wished for more mathematics, more mathematics than we got at our classics- and literature-focused high school, which I had chosen to attend because anything ancient has always taken precedence for me, even over numbers—a fixation that has been among the many sources of my misfortune. I would have liked to be able to reassure that little boy, tell him he could cling to that sliver of truth forever, but the reality is, there isn't enough mathematics in the world.

I turned toward Tommaso, who had arrived shortly after me and sat beside me. I did not remember the clothes he had worn last week, but I could have sworn it was the same outfit. He listened to Sara with no expression. He did not seem bored, or lost, or perturbed. He seemed untouched by emotion, like the thick waters of an artificial lake. Her story about the little boy wasn't exactly going anywhere, anyway. Just another attempt to convince us we weren't alone.

Sara read some other stories aloud, but none of them seemed to have an ending. A parade of nameless, voiceless children we would never meet, and whose present we would never discover, either—whether they'd recovered, whether they had learned to overcome their trauma, whether they'd started talking again. I knew that we all wanted to ask the same question, but the downside of mutism is that even the right kind of question cannot be uttered, and instead you have to wait for life to provide the answer, even though life, unlike people, is never in a rush, and, a bit like people, it tends to forget about things and let them go.

Sara announced that we would be joined the following week by a guest who would talk to us about his experience. Someone who, like us, had lived in silence for many years, then emerged on the other side. I can't imagine there's anything trickier than running a support group for people who won't express themselves; you'd either need to have logorrhea or possess powers of imagination similar to those of children who throw tea parties for their dolls. That day the meeting ended five minutes earlier than scheduled, and we all stood up at once to leave.

Tommaso had walked out before me and was smoking a cigarette. I went to stand next to him and he offered me one, displaying what looked like a half smile. We smoked together while the others made their way to their cars or their bicycles, nodding goodbye as they went past us, but we did not respond. How long does a lit cigarette last? Silvia and I had worked it out once: anywhere between two to six minutes, depending on the weather and the frequency and strength with which you inhaled. On particularly windy days, you might barely make it to a minute, but we rarely had days like that in Turin. Tommaso's cigarette seemed never-ending. I stubbed mine out on the big standing ashtray in the corner of the portico; then Tommaso started walking toward his car and I followed him. When we were halfway there, he stopped, turned around, and stared at me. He couldn't ask me anything, and I couldn't explain. All I could do was walk up to him and take his hand. It was rigid but warm. I put my hand back in my pocket and he started walking toward his car again. He made room for me on the passenger seat, which was covered with plastic envelopes and bits of paper, some scattered and others grouped into color-coded folders. They might have been related to his work, the nature of which I would never discover. He tossed everything onto the backseat before I could make out any of the writing.

I realized that spending time with other practitioners of silence bored me because it made it impossible to play Clue with their lives. I had always enjoyed uncovering a person's story through the clues scattered in the things they said. I hated asking personal questions because I hated it when people did it to me, so I limited myself to reconstructing their lives piece by piece, using my imagination to glue the parts together and—when I got something right—rewarding myself with phantom points that didn't amount to anything. This was a much more absorbing activity than asking questions out of courtesy and having to listen to the interminable responses they provoked. I missed it a little bit. I hadn't had much of a chance to meet new people whose lives I could speculate about. Perhaps I could go and sit on a bench, in a park or at the bus stop, and wait to be approached by a talkative stranger. Though, unfortunately, the kinds of people who most feel the need to share also tend to have the least interesting stories.

Tommaso drove out of the parking lot and onto the main road, then turned confidently onto Unione Sovietica Avenue and followed it all the way to Lingotto. I knew that neighborhood because of a concert venue named Hiroshima Mon Amour and a public library—named after a German theologian—that I had ended up using a few times to consult some texts I needed for my thesis. The library building was in the brutalist style and resembled the spaceship from *Close Encounters of the Third Kind*. Or the mouth of a whale, due to a series of concrete brise-soleils that looked like a row of baleen plates. The grimy concrete gave the building a derelict appearance, which contrasted nicely with the lushness of the park that surrounded it and the glass façade of the ground floor. Obsolescence and futurism, like in a low budget sci-fi movie. I used to come home from afternoons spent in those rooms, sliced through horizontally by the dying light, with themed DVDs I had borrowed, like *Nineteen Eighty-Four* or *Soylent Green*. It was a shame that my application for state-run voluntary service had been rejected and I'd had to resign myself to working in my local library, housed in a pretentious little villa from the 1700s that tended, rather boringly, to be universally praised.

Tommaso stopped the car in a residential parking lot outside a gray-and-blue building, one of those oversized and anonymous apartment blocks like the one my parents had chosen, which reminded you at every turn that you were in a city of factory workers. He got out of the car and I followed him. The lobby had matchboard paneling and the lift was made of metal, so that the whole place looked like one of those serviced apartments you found up in the mountains sometimes, still stuck in the 1970s. There were eight floors; Tommaso pressed the button for the seventh. The lift made an infernal racket, but I was not afraid. I thought of the anechoic chamber again and wondered if the opposite might also exist, a discombobulating place teeming with such noise as to prompt the human beings inside it to emit some kind of sound themselves, if only to reaffirm their existence and not be entirely annihilated.

Tommaso led the way down mirrored, matchboard-lined hallways and opened his door. The apartment was a spacious loft with large curtainless windows, freshly redecorated, the floors and the furniture all off-white. He was growing marijuana in one of the rooms, and you could smell it even through the closed door. He kept the plants under HID lamps that lit up the room as if the Madonna herself had landed on earth, like a temple devoted to a plant god. He started rolling a joint and I pressed my forehead against the window, pulled back, then got up close again to check how far down I could see. From that height, the suburbs looked like an abstract painting, the work of some mad artist who had poured a dark color over everything, then set about scattering it with yellow dots to feel less alone.

We smoked without looking at each other, then fucked on a

futon—or perhaps it was merely a mattress on the floor—with navy blue linen sheets, taking care not to make a sound even in the most salient moments. I thought of Silvia, remembered what she'd said about Davide's heart, and concluded that Tommaso probably didn't have one at all, as I couldn't hear it even if I concentrated. Maybe he just had lungs that requested he breathe every now and then, and that he obliged by discreetly sucking some air in, like when you take a soft drink to the theater. There was only the sound of our bodies moving in the room, the voice of the furniture and the bedsheets. Not us. We were nothing.

We smoked again; then I got dressed and went to stand by the front door, like a pet that wants to be let out.

THE NEXT DAY my alarm clock pulled me out of a very deep sleep. I had a headache and briefly convinced myself that I must have died and come back to life during the night. I hadn't slept this much in months, maybe years. I tried to get out of bed, but my forehead seemed to be caving into my skull, so I wrote another message to say I would not be coming into work. I didn't care anymore. I tried to eat something to soothe the pain in and around my chest, but I couldn't get anything down. I could only drink water, and my liquid-filled stomach seemed to amplify my distress. It wasn't exactly pain I was feeling—more a sensation of emptiness and simultaneously of acute awareness, as if I could feel the location of each of my internal organs as they executed their functions, but did so in slow motion. Maybe they had grown tired.

It was an awful and unrelenting feeling, and for a moment I was tempted to stick my hand down my throat to pull my esophagus out and drag all the rest of my digestive system with it. I was convinced I could do it, as if my esophagus and stomach were the tab on a protective sleeve or an unwanted hair so thick I could pluck it out with my fingernails. I could feel my chest catching fire and wanted to scream and beg God or whoever was in charge to make it stop.

But I couldn't scream, and even if I had, God or whoever was in charge wouldn't have listened, so instead I did the only thing I knew could rescue me from moments like those, which was to put a random song on repeat and let it play at least ten times. It couldn't be anything upbeat, because when you're sad, it can be hard to put up with happiness, and it couldn't be anything too fast either, lest that should awaken other feelings—because as Giacomo had once told me, when pain comes looking for you, you need to stop and swallow it whole; otherwise it'll come back and find you in your sleep. I clicked on the playlist I had prepared for this kind of situation and the shuffle function picked Nirvana's "Something in the Way." When the song said it's okay to eat fish 'cause they don't have any feelings, I turned toward Harpo, hoping he would somehow return my gaze. I was sure that as well as shrimp, Harpo also fed on feelings, and so this apartment was just perfect for him. My body exuded emotions, and the silence was a sauna.

Had I been brave enough, I would have admitted to being moved by the same motive as Kurt Cobain. I would have liked to end things in the same way, but I was too proud and too proper to admit it, and not strong enough to go through with it. So instead I had resorted to a series of minor limitations, which only served to draw more attention to myself, like those children who are used to receiving attention and so have no qualms about screaming over nothing, just as a newborn might do. I thought of those stories you hear about people who jump off buildings, buildings so tall you'd have time to regret it as you fell, with your life flashing before your eyes, hidden memories, redemption and light—and that last breath where your lungs expand a little more than necessary, to take their fill of the world and then let go. I made an effort to think about the things I would regret if I happened to be on the verge of death. I thought about films. Not all of them, just a few. I thought of the Nike of Samothrace and the Rosetta Stone. The Giza Necropolis, which I would never get to see. The autumn, which would come round without me. I thought of snow. Of ice. Of great bodies of water—God knows why humans are so attracted to bodies of water. I thought of the letter I had written when I was eight years old, addressed to the house in which we then lived, telling her that I would have wanted to be like her, a solid, stable creature made solely out of her inhabitants' emotions, with no soul and no heart, and expressing herself through nothing but sighs and creaks. I remembered how I had hidden the letter in a gap in the baseboard and hadn't managed to get it out again, and now it would stay there, with the new owners, never to be found again.

I looked at Harpo and at the reflections of the water onto the walls and of the cars onto the street, like alien forms whose lives ran parallel to ours. I focused on my legs and my feet and the bones under my skin; I focused on the space my veins and muscles occupied for as long as my lungs let me breathe. Then I watched *The Social Network* for the three hundredth time on the DVD Daniele had never claimed back, and I thought that this was going to be the most I would get out of this day, and that this feeling of nothingness was, at any rate, better than nothingness itself.

Dear Silvia,

I am writing this letter because I need to talk to you.

Sometimes I daydream of coming to your house and buzzing your intercom, saying nothing and hoping you'll figure out it's me, waiting for you to come down and admit it's not a problem if I don't say anything, not anymore, because you're like all those other people who see it as a gift to them, a chance to talk without being interrupted or judged, to talk about themselves without pause, as deep down everyone feels like they're special and craves nothing more than to be noticed.

But you're not like those other people.

I will not come to your house. I already tried that with Daniele, and it was a disaster. I ended up hiding in the entrance to the basement area—can you believe it?

These days I'm remembering many things. Things that take the form of vinyl records, of gray afternoons, of waking up and needing something savory to soak up the night before, of plastic bottles on the floor, endless plastic bottles on the floor, someone will eventually have the energy to get rid of them, of glasses of cold milk and Nesquik, of frozen pizzas and cookies, who says we need to distinguish between savory and sweet. Sometimes I pour myself a glass of milk and try to find the same taste again, but I've had it too often and it tastes different now. The problem is that in our brains, useless moments live in the same rooms as important ones, and they contaminate each other. You never know which memory will torment you on any given day—something insignificant, or a happy moment you wish you could relive, or an unpleasant one to cause you anguish.

That's what I've come to realize over these past few months.

Memories are on shuffle play, and there's nothing you can do to control them. It's an aspect of silence I hadn't considered. Cleansing yourself of spoken words, of the effort of having to choose the right ones, means you end up being tortured by all the wrong ones.

Sometimes I feel like I can't do anything at all. The better I get at stopping words, the more I hold on to everything else. It's like in "Donnie Darko": I can see the projection of future movement. But that projection is all there is of the movement, like a prophecy that won't come true. They're small liquid trails, like in the film, small waves that won't leave me alone. But there are other times when I think that I am doing the right thing. If I still have so many uneasy thoughts, so many soiled words inside me, it must mean I haven't recovered yet. Do you remember Agnese from high school (I wonder what she's doing now?), who didn't know what to do about her acne and was persuaded to try that healer? The healer prescribed her some kind of concoction, and when the pimples, rather than disappearing, actually increased in number, the healer claimed it was the natural course of the treatment, because acne originated in the liver and the liver needed purifying—"purging," she'd actually said—and the impurities always passed through the skin. Maybe that's what's happening to me, maybe this is the time for my mind to fry so that it can free and cleanse itself, and these thoughts are just the ghosts of the words I misspoke in the past, the right words I held in, the awful ones I pictured other people saying whenever I felt I was being judged.

Agnese's mother eventually found out what she was doing, remember? She made her get rid of the concoction and we were a little disappointed because we never found out whether the treatment worked. Well, now that I've started my own treatment, I want to know if it works. I bet you're curious, too.

I wanted to tell you that I think of you often, because as you can see, I'm very good at thinking, too. Will my mind ever give up? Maybe it's like you said. We're not human if we don't communicate, and this letter proves that point. In the end there is one thing I can't seem to give up: complaining. I feel increasingly like the cat in that meme, the one where he is sitting by the window wondering why he's so alone, and when a human approaches to stroke him, he swats them away. I suppose you have always told me I must have been a cat in my past life.

I dream a lot, and I often see you in my dreams. I can still talk and we are still only seventeen. You call me Martinez, slurring the "z" so that it sounds like an "s." You do my eye makeup on Saturday nights because I don't know how. Boys are both a recurring topic and a temporary diversion, and we never get too attached. We are foolish and happy, though unaware of being either. Sometimes I want to

I left the letter unfinished and eventually ripped it up. But first I stopped to study it for a moment. Not to reread what I had written, but to notice how my handwriting was the same as it had been in high school. Without practice, it had frozen in time. I tore the letter into tiny pieces, like confetti or even smaller, then mixed them up with Harpo's feed and spread the mixture all across the surface of the water. I spent the first few minutes religiously observing his toothy mouth tearing my words up, and the next ones googling *Do fish die if they eat paper?*

It seemed no one had thought to ask that question before.

July

SOMETHING WEIRD HAPPENED. A young woman stopped me in one of the corridors of the library and asked me if I would be willing to answer some questions. I thought it must be a survey, some kind of study on quality of life, the university, politics, all things I no longer had anything to do with. I looked into her eyes and hoped she'd understand that I couldn't respond. She said: "I know you can't talk. I've printed them out for you."

She handed me a piece of paper folded into quarters. "If you want, you can write your answers underneath. I'm sorry to ambush you like this—I wasn't trying to corner you. I asked the department for your email address but they wouldn't give it to me, I guess due to privacy concerns, which makes sense. I looked for you on social media, but I couldn't find you. Take as much time as you need; you don't have to answer all of them either. I've put my email address on there, so if you email me I can send you the file—whatever you prefer. Otherwise you can find me in the library every afternoon except on Mondays, all the way through to the summer session. I like studying here better than at home," she said, smiling. "My parents can be a little interfering."

She spoke fast and gesticulated furiously. She told me she was twenty-three years old and studying philosophy. She was small, so that I needed to tilt my chin down to look at her. She wore thick glasses with black frames, and her nose was a little squashed and wide at the tip, like those rag dolls with buttons sewn into the middle of their faces.

"I come here a lot—I don't know if you've ever seen me. Probably not, but it doesn't matter, I'm used to that. You see, I think you and I have a lot in common. I know you're not mute, and that at some point you stopped talking. I don't want to seem nosy—it's not that I want to know your business. It's just that, well, if your silence is a choice, then I'd like to know more about it. I think it's a very brave choice to make, at this particular moment. I would love to talk to you about it, though I suppose *talking* is not the right word," she said, giggling. "That's why I'm giving you this. I put loads of questions on there, probably too many, it's just that I don't know anything about you or about your motivations. If any of the questions seem stupid or pointless or misleading, don't reply, and feel free to cross them out. But I would love to know a little more about your story, if you're up for it. Whatever you feel comfortable telling me. I think it could be of great help to me, right now."

She suddenly stopped, just as I had begun to fear she never would. She giggled again, then looked down. I thought she might crouch into a ball and roll off in the same way as she had arrived. She had the barest trace of a gap tooth, which made her look rather sexy, and I wondered if she'd ever noticed. She apologized for the tenth time and waved goodbye, pointing at the piece of paper she had given me before walking away along the bile-colored linoleum floor, against which her shoes, just like everyone's shoes, squeaked at every step.

Back home, I kept turning the piece of paper around in my hands, but couldn't face unfolding it. If I threw it away without looking at the questions, it would be easier to forget the whole thing; I simply wouldn't turn up at work and that girl would never see me again. She would forget me and I would forget her and everything would go back to normal. One thing I had learned from the relatively brief yet infinite time I had spent on this earth was that the amount of worry we feel about the possible consequences of something is inversely proportional to how long its memory will endure. The things that torment us are the ones we least expect.

I went to place the sheet on the table, like they do in the movies when an important letter has arrived, a college admissions letter in a coming-of-age comedy. In those scenes they usually prop the letter up, lean it against a vase of flowers or a jug of water. I owned neither of those objects, and my piece of paper was not a letter that was going to change my life but an annoying parasite that had insinuated itself into the life I had carefully and laboriously curated in the service of silence and anonymity. So I flung the sheet onto the table without any theatrical flourishes and hoped it would just disappear. I could have torn it up and fed it to Harpo, but afterward I was likely to end up doing something to compensate—smoking a cigarette, picking at my cuticles, pouring myself a glass of water from the tap just to hear the sound, then drinking half of it because I felt thirsty and tipping the rest into the sink—and so the sheet of questions stayed where it was, staring at me. It was nearly eight in the evening and there was no sign of the heat diminishing or the sun retreating. I rolled the blinds up completely and stared at the building across the street. Some windows were closed but I could see people moving behind the curtains, picture them safe and cool in their air-conditioned rooms, making distracted conversation as they sat in front of the evening news on TV. I opened the freezer and pulled out a frozen pizza to put in the oven. I would have it with a beer and a glass of whiskey with ice cream for dessert, and I would let myself be swaddled by the heat until it became yet another simulation of death.

But that's not what happened. What happened instead was that I woke up around three, on the sofa, with the TV still on, playing a very old underground film that had been ruined in the conversion to digital, all the voices croaky and the colors burned. I finished my glass of whiskey, the melted ice cream mixing with the alcohol and turning it into a sort of medicine that needed to be taken and that resembled a galaxy if you stopped to look, and then I sat at the table. In the half hour that followed, I filled out the questionnaire. I tried to be brief even though the words were jostling inside of me, eager to get out, like flies that had gone crazy from being shut away for too long. No more than two sentences per question, no more than one lie per answer. I used up the last fragments of semi-sober attention I had left, placed an enormous period at the end of my last response—which was longer and more honest than the others, and made me feel exposed—and finally dragged myself to bed, like a wild animal driven out of its den and looking for shelter.

I RETURNED THE questionnaire three days later, during the afternoon shift. The full stop I'd put at the end was so heavy that it had made a hole in the paper. My handwriting was practically illegible. I didn't dwell on any of that. When I came back from lunch, the girl was sitting at her table, so I slid the paper in front of her and returned to my desk before she could say anything. I hated her, and hated myself for having fallen for it.

THE SELF-HELP GROUP was on summer break. The last meeting had been as Sara had promised us: a young man who, like her, had traveled through the dark tunnel of selective mutism and come out the other end. It was an interminable hour: the guy spoke at a rate of one word every ten seconds, and it was impossible to follow what he was saying. The logic connecting each sentence to the next grew increasingly flimsy, and his syntax was precarious. I wondered whether I too would struggle to talk, if and when I should decide to end the silence. People always say that foreign languages can be forgotten, that it's not like riding a bike. Could the same be true of language itself?

I was so bored that I started thinking about Erica, the girl who had given me the piece of paper with the questions, and I pictured her as a scientist in disguise. Maybe she was a member of a research group focusing on the long-term effects of self-induced mutism and wanted to learn if it was possible to unlearn how to speak. My nonsensical responses would confirm her thesis. Within a few days I was bound to find myself lying on an operating table, surrounded by aspiring young neuroscientists who were about to slice my head open in search of synapses that would confirm there was permanent damage. They would be covered in glory, while I would end up like a lab rat—no need for a lobotomy, as I had performed one on myself.

I was brought back to life by Sara, who took over to thank the guy and announce the end of the hour. I leapt to my feet and went straight outside. Out of the corner of my eye I could see Tommaso watching me. I hurried back home, on foot, thinking that in some respects I must have gotten worse, because I could no longer stand people who talked too slowly. When I wasn't at home, everything bored me. Perhaps by imposing rest on the part of my brain that was dedicated to language I had given more space to the other parts. Perhaps the language part was already being swallowed up by all the others and would soon be left permanently atrophied, as was clearly the case with the young man Sara had invited. When I got home, I fed Harpo, lay on the sofa, switched on the TV, and stopped worrying about my brain.

So the self-help group had been put on hold, and the following week I felt empty, like Marla Singer when she gets found out. At work I'd come to a kind of agreement with Patrizia. By now she was sure that I had lied to her, but—as someone must have suggested to her—she had also convinced herself that my mutism must be the consequence of some kind of shock I'd experienced, and so she had become compassionate again. She no longer tried to push me. We'd reached precisely the degree of automation and lack of participatory drive to which I had aspired.

With the summer sessions over, the university was emptying out, and in August it would close down completely. Perhaps I should go away somewhere too, just as I imagined my classmates must be doing. Probably following their families, who would spend the whole time worrying about them when all their children really wanted was to be left in peace. Every now and then I pictured myself buying a random ticket from among the day's offers, clicking the "I'm flexible" button on Airbnb, and picking somewhere unusual to stay in, like a tiny hut at the North Pole or a historic building in a far-flung French village—any kind of place where I could get lost, where nobody would recognize me, and with the language barrier acting as an excuse for my lack of communication. I would subsist on local produce bought from grocery stores or markets, gesturing with my head, pointing at things. I've always admired people who have the courage to practice what they preach. To separate from society without hurting anyone, without going off to set up neo-Nazi groups, as is the habit of people who claim to hate society. When really, it's just that society doesn't agree with them on everything—as often happens to assholes. Sometimes one who thinks himself incomplete is merely an asshole. Is that how Italo Calvino put it? I would have liked to call Silvia to check.

And to ask her: Have I become an asshole, too?

Acts

Hi, I'm Erica and I'm majoring in philosophy.

Please find below a series of questions. Don't worry, I'm not planning to write a thesis about this :) It's just my own curiosity, as I've heard people talking about you in the corridors and have become interested in your case. I really admire the choice you've made and I would like to know more about it, but I promise I'll keep your answers to myself.

I've put down all the questions I could think of. There might be repetitions or similarities, and if any of them seem inappropriate, feel free to skip them or cross them out.

Thank you for taking the time to respond to my questions (should you decide to do so).

1) How old are you?
Twenty-nine.

2) What is your occupation?
Archive librarian.

3) What did you study?
Futile things.

4) Were you born here or did you move here?
Born.

5) How long has it been since you stopped talking?
Nearly six months.

6) When did you make this decision?
Six months ago.

~~7) What made you do it?~~
~~*It's a question I often ask myself.*~~

8) Was there a last straw?
I don't think so. It was a need that developed over time, a little like needing to poop.

9) Did you stop gradually or at all once?
At once.

10) Did you warn anyone? And if so, who was the first person you told?
—

11) Do you have other means of communicating with people? Do you write?
Only when strictly necessary. And 99.9% of the time, it isn't.

12) Do you live alone or with anyone else?
I live with myself and that's one too many.

13) Are you seeing anyone? And if so, have they tried to change your mind?
I'm not.

14) What is your relationship with your parents? What do they make of your decision?

They're dead.

15) How did you inform your boss of this change? Did they give you trouble?
No.

16) What do you miss the most of your previous life?
Nothing.

17) And what do you think you might have gained?
I'm less impulsive.

18) Do you think you'll start talking again? If yes, have you given yourself a time limit?
I haven't thought about that yet.

19) Since you stopped communicating, have you ever "slipped"?
Once. Twice, including now.

20) Are there any special circumstances that might cause you to put your silence "on hold"?
I haven't thought about it.

21) What's the hardest thing about silence?
Not talking.

22) What's the best part?
Indifference.

23) Would you consider yourself more of an introvert or an extrovert?
An extrovert.

24) Do you have many friends?
No.

25) Do you believe in God? Are you religious?
I'd like to be.

26) What are your passions?
My favorite is silence.

27) Ever since you began, how have you been spending your days?
At the mercy of my needs, just like any living being.

28) Do you have children? Would you like any?
People have children out of boredom or out of some extreme form of self-love. Both emotions I am not familiar with.

29) Do you like animals?
Yes.

30) Do you like people?
Too much and not enough.

31) How is your relationship with social media?
Conflicted.

32) If you could teleport to another historical period, which one would you choose?
The past. Doesn't matter when.

—

7) What made you do it?
The happiest time of my life was when I expressed myself through inarticulate sounds. I am fairly certain that the trouble starts where language begins.

August

THE CITY EMPTIED OUT and my parents went to the seaside with Elena and Elia. They called me every other day to check that I hadn't killed myself or suffocated in my sleep; I picked up the phone and listened to them talk, breathing loudly so that they would know I still existed. With nobody else around, I could be the worst version of myself twenty-four hours a day, uninterruptedly. I wondered sometimes if there was a limit to how bad that worst version could be or if it was a bottomless pit. This new version of me included late afternoon walks, dodging the thunderstorms, whose habits were the same as mine. I had stopped using clocks, following instead the rhythms of the natural world. I walked down the same streets I had been down a thousand times before and tried to cleanse them of any memories, just as the city had done with its inhabitants.

THE GIRL WITH the questionnaire hadn't held up her end of the bargain. But I didn't blame her; I hadn't held up my end either. I tried to atone by hurting myself every day. Small daily helpings of pain, like an amateur fakir. I would only pick movies I had previously seen with Giacomo and would watch them five times in a row, until they lost any meaning, like words do when they are repeated too many times. I would chew on ice cubes instead of gummy bears, and eventually instead of food as well. After the first few times, my gums stopped complaining, but I did need the toilet more often. The ice soothed my throat and kept me full, and it was cold and pure. I watched films on DVD, avoiding live TV and keeping my computer off. I had stopped looking at the news because I felt like it was always about me. If a man had stabbed his wife to death, it was about me. If a child had gone missing, it was about me. If a hurricane destroyed a city on the other side of the world, it was about me. I walked and drank ice-cold water and tried to find again the emptiness I had lost. If I needed nothing, then I could be nothing. "What's going on?" Elena would ask me from the other end of the telephone line. "Is it you they're talking about?" I listened to her voice while blowing smoke out the window, the rooftops gleaming in the wet light of a necessary malaise.

Dear Elena,

This is how it all began, and how I would like it to continue. I was about to write "end," because I suppose in some ways it is an end, but actually it's more like the deepest phase, and the truest.

This will be my last letter, the last thing I ever write. I started this "thing" (I don't know what else to call it: a journey? That sounds so formulaic and spiritual) in a fairly automatic way. I could feel that I had nothing important to say, and all the unimportant words I pronounced kept coming back at me like a freak wave. By the end of the day I was always exhausted, not from hearing but from speaking, and I could feel everything around me rushing at supersonic speed, leaving me out of breath when I tried to keep up. So I stopped. I just wanted to recover a little. I was managing, too, but I guess life is unpredictable and finds some way to climb in through your window, whether you like it or not. And the last thing I want is for everything to stop and for people to start talking about me. I didn't slow down so that the world would sit and wait for me. I didn't ask to be understood, or to be consoled, or indeed emulated. I still feel that possessiveness toward small discoveries that we tend to develop in middle school, when the experience of a friend copying the way you dressed would flatter you at first, until it started bothering you. And I've never enjoyed sharing my passions. I guess you knew that already.

I feel like Forrest Gump, when all those journalists are asking him why he's been running for so long, what is he trying to prove, what is he protesting against, and all he says is: I just felt like running.

Well, I just felt like being silent. The point is, I've failed, I've not been silent enough. It's the hardest thing I've ever done, you know? Your whole body starts rebelling, urging you to do what you don't want to do, a little like when you're on a diet and you start dreaming of cream puffs. It's just like those modern-day weirdo hippies say, the kind who hole up in countryside retreats to do yoga, cleanse their colons, and stop talking for a while. I'd always thought that hunger and self-deception must have something to do with it, but now I can see that they were right all along. You end up taking your thoughts back and—rather unexpectedly—your memories, too. Your mind turns into a flow of images from the past, and yes, in case you were wondering, it does feel like torture at first, but eventually—it's a bit weird when you try to explain it—past and present stop being two distinct entities, and that's reassuring. That's how I imagine what the last few moments before death must feel like. There's something redemptive in all this, though I have yet to discover what. But I can feel that I'm close.

Now, as well as being silent, I'll have to disappear, too. I'll be away for a little while. I'll leave Harpo with you—please take care of him for me. He doesn't need much, only to be fed every two days (you'll find his food on the cupboard next to the fish tank) and to be left alone, in his crevices. If you tap on the glass too much, he gets scared, so please don't do that. Once he gets used to your presence and understands that you're not a danger to him, you'll start seeing him come out of his den more. You could even teach Elia to take care of him; I'm sure he'd be really good at it.

I'll discreetly send you signals so that you know I'm well. I'll figure out a way.

Please don't show this letter to anyone. Maybe you could tear it up. But please don't feed it to Harpo, as I've discovered that scorpionfish aren't supposed to eat paper.

Yours, all of you,
C.

Dear Daniele,

You've written me four letters over these past few months, twelve pages in total, which I reread whenever I need to feel less alone and less distant, but to which I have never responded, though I am doing so now to tell you once more that I will not speak to you again. How can you not hate me? Perhaps by now you've learned how. I hope so.

Once again, and in a totally selfish manner, I am denying you what you deserve to have. I'm taking what I have no right to take, the pleasure of spending time with you, though in this incomplete and somewhat juvenile way I've made up, and in exchange I give you something useless that you didn't even ask for.

You met me at a very strange time in my life, and if you'd seen "Fight Club" enough times, you'd know what I'm referring to. But the fact that you haven't seen it, or didn't pay enough attention to it, is something I ought to have appreciated more. I'm stupid and ungrateful and I deserve to disappear together with this fiction I have created. You don't belong in it. That's all I wanted to say to you. You've been the one real thing in my life during these past few months. I was trying to recover some form of truth and I found it in you, only I never realized that. I wasted it, and so I deserve to end up in the circle of hell reserved for selfish people, where the law of the counterpoise will leave them alone for eternity, at the mercy of memories, which, bit by bit, will devour their minds.

Harpo is still there, though. Sometimes I feel like he can't stand me either, and I start to wonder whether fish ever commit suicide. Do they poke their heads out until they suffocate? Do they fight the instinct to dive back into the water? Who knows if I'll ever learn the answer. In the meantime, I've found a few lines I had written in a notebook in September last year, before you and I met. Reading them again now, they sound so pathetic that they almost make me laugh, but I've decided to show them to you because I do think that, in spite of everything, they contain something of me, and maybe after all this time you do actually deserve something that isn't totally superficial. I've pasted them below. I would have liked to leave you with something funny, too, but it'll have to wait until another life.

Thank you for the effort you put into showing me you're not like all the people I'm describing below. Myself included. And I'm sorry.

C.

If I had a wish, I'd waste it like this: I'd ask for everyone to be like me. Poor, like me. Inept, like me. Selfish, like me. Spineless, like me. Soulless, like me. With nothing to say, like me.

If I had another, it would be like this: I'd wish that people would stop talking, that everyone would just be quiet. Because I'm tired of being disappointed. Every word leads to another, and another, and every one of them will, eventually, break your heart.

PART TWO

E.

In the future, everyone will be anonymous for fifteen minutes.

—ANONYMOUS

(LATER QUOTED BY BANKSY)

Propagation

These days I only believe in C. We've killed words, we pulled them toward us when we needed them, then tore them up and tossed them away, we used them to define who we are, then threw them in the faces of our perceived enemies, of anybody who didn't agree with us. The purpose we first began to use words for, the act of sharing, has long since been undermined. It is no longer the aim. So we find that in the midst of this uncontrollable torrent of neologisms, labels, asterisks, and declinations, which—rather than forms of inclusion—seem to me like pretexts for new schisms (or like instruments of power, used by those who wield power against those who never will), C. decides to strip herself of it all and abstain from words, all words, without exception. I admire her and I feel feeble and hypocritical for my inability to do the same. I admire her like a meat-eating animal lover admires a vegan. Like a serial sinner praying every day for salvation. Every day she makes me face up to my indecision.

These days it seems like people just can't wait to take a side. But I think that intelligence and common sense can also be measured through the ways we choose not to say anything.

If you think about it, any person of average intelligence is always wearing a mask. They recognize this as a necessity, and change the tone of their voice and their vocabulary and what they show of themselves according to the context they're in. The only people who are always the same are those who live at the extremes: either they're very stupid or they're very intelligent. C. undoubtedly belongs in the second category. But she takes things one step further: she remains identical to herself, without offering any grounds for critique, without generating any kind of discussion. Her silence neither denies debate nor fuels it. She does not feed off it either. By saying nothing, she says the realest thing. She doesn't lie to anyone. She doesn't lie to herself.

The point is that our words hold whatever meaning others decide to attribute to them, and everything can be distorted and decontextualized and weaponized. Without words we are nobody: and I want to embrace that nobody, be voiceless, without thoughts, without a name, like when you've just come out of the womb and every possibility is open to you; you aren't anything yet so you can be anything, you're light and truth without name or consciousness.

Try watching a movie, going to the theater, or reading a book you find particularly memorable, whether in a good or a bad way. Go to a trendy restaurant, buy yourself an item of clothing you've been coveting for a while. Take a trip to an exotic destination. Now try not to talk to anyone about it. Keep the whole experience to yourself, don't share anything about it, force yourself to avoid the subject, even when you're asked about it directly. It'll feel unnatural and mean. Even as the whole world has something to talk about, you will be choosing silence.

That's the life C. has been leading for almost a year. We are not aware of her precise identity; we know that she is nearly thirty years old, lives in Turin, and that, for many months now, she has devoted her life to silence. Not a single word, spoken or written, not even with the people she is closest to. And it is a fully considered choice.

Her case has become publicly known ever since some young people began posting on Reddit to make their own vows of silence, inspired by an interview with C., which has since been taken offline, where the young woman claimed not to have spoken in months and to have benefited greatly from this decision. The hashtag #silence has gone viral; on TikTok, trends such as "communicational minimalism" and "relational decluttering" encourage users to embrace quietude and solitude, and to oppose unabashed sharing. In these clips, which contain no sound, these young people are motionless, either meditating or simply staring straight ahead, with captions like "This is the last video I will post." There is also a countercurrent that is harshly critical of C.'s followers, noting how dangerous the absence of communication can be, and how important it is to make one's voice heard, particularly when faced with injustice or abuses of power. Psychologists and therapists are using their own accounts to offer appointments and free support, with the slogan "The only way forward is to talk about it." Yet the circle of silence seems to grow ever wider, increasingly involving older people, too, in a trend that is unheeding of generational boundaries. This trend increasingly seems to be acquiring the contours of a movement. After Facebook, is this the new revolution?

The real news is to find a woman who can be quiet for longer than a minute hahahahaha

Of all the vows you can make—if we can even call it a vow, given that C. and her followers profess to be atheists—it is one of the hardest to keep, even harder than fasting. Man is a social animal, and if he begins to feel he is not contributing anything to society, not even his own narrative of it, he will begin to die. Yet C. resists, doggedly loyal to her vow. Like a strange kind of crusader, she fights a solitary battle she will not name. She chooses silence over conviviality. She chooses mystery over display, reserve over ostentatiousness. And she turns this into something so radical that it becomes a form of art. It is as if she were saying: Look at me. I exist by virtue of myself.

We didn't care about words at all, before, but now we understand that they are crucial. Before, they were a necessary instrument, but now it's like walking in a minefield. For years we have been planting explosive devices on arable land needed for survival, and now every time we make use of that land, we risk losing a hand, an arm, an eye. We live in fear.

Read this: "The first level of wisdom is knowing how to be silent, the second is knowing how to express many ideas in a few words, the third is knowing how to speak without saying too much and badly. You should only speak when you have something to say that is truly worth it, or, at least, worth more than silence." Hernán Huarache Mamani
In order to know how to be silent, there must first be a phase of total fasting, in which the body can free itself of all the residue left behind by words and by the negative emotions they entail.

if we're not allowed to say anything anymore, it's better to be silent
you wanted us pacified, now we will be mute

there is no shame in giving up
silence makes us equal

Don't you realize that words stopped being our friends ages ago? They stopped being useful to us, and all they do now is divide us and pit us against one another. Anytime we seek to reconcile things, we are defeated. We keep going round in circles without ever making sense of it. But the trouble starts where language begins. A total ban is the only solution.

I think that detoxing from words must be like swimming, like emerging again from the baptismal font, without sin and with all your life ahead of you.

I'm starting tonight; wish me luck.

Evangelization

I DON'T KNOW where she is. I don't even know why she decided to do what she did. She wrote me a letter, the one you've seen. I don't know anything else. She said she made her mind up after thinking about it for many days, but she never told us anything about it. She's always been like that. She doesn't know this, as she was too young to remember, but when she was three years old she broke her arm and for two days, nobody knew. She was at preschool when she slipped and fell out of a tree—that's what the teacher told us. Nobody saw her fall; they found her when she was already on the ground and struggling to get up, and she wouldn't tell anybody what had happened. My sister started talking when she was nine months old. She could express herself fully at the age of one and a half, but she only did so with us or with her teachers. She always picked adults; she did not speak to those her own age. By the time she was three, she had no trouble communicating, yet she insisted on not talking about her accident. I was almost nine years old so I can remember it, how she replied just by shaking her head or nodding, and there was a chance someone had pushed her out on purpose, but now we will never know.

Anyway, my parents didn't take her to the emergency room, because she was walking fine and had no visible injuries other than a scraped knee, a little scratch on her elbow, and dirt on her dress. In the evening she behaved as she always did: she ate her food, she talked about everything except what had happened, almost as if she were ashamed of it. It was me who noticed, two days later, that something was wrong; it was a Sunday and we were playing in the yard—she was running around and I was trying to catch her; I grabbed her arm and she let out a shriek as if she'd been burned. I had been gentle, I was sure of it, and she was not like one of those little girls who scream at the drop of a hat. I think I must have heard her crying only three times in my life, and even when she was a newborn, my parents say she barely made a fuss when she was hungry. So I got scared and looked at her arm, the bruise was pretty big, and as I held her still and peered at it, I could see her grimacing and holding back tears. I told my parents and we went to the emergency room; it was broken in two places. They put her arm in a cast, and she still looked like she was embarrassed about it. Whatever my mother must have told her then evidently did not stick. I've never understood her passion for silence—I'm the opposite, and so is my mother. Whenever I find myself in a room with people I don't know and nothing else to do, like in a waiting room, for example, I get agitated. To me, silence feels like the antechamber of death.

Did she go through episodes of mutism when she was little? No, not that. I wouldn't say she was a silent child. Reserved, perhaps, and certainly quiet, very mature for her age—she would rarely interrupt the grown-ups on a whim, just to get their attention. But she never had trouble talking in front of strangers, or in the classroom, when she was called upon to do so. She did go through a lying phase, though. This was in primary school, fourth or fifth grade. First she only did it with her classmates; then she started with us, too. At school she would tell people she'd been to Disneyland or to the U.S. to explain why she had been absent for five days, when the truth was, she'd merely had the flu. Conversely, if our parents decided to keep us out of school for a couple of days after the weekend, just so we could spend a little more time visiting our grandparents, she would say that she had ended up in hospital with appendicitis or food poisoning. That kind of thing.

To us, she'd say that the teacher had organized a number of cultural outings, and then she'd have my parents sign a permission form. What she did with those signatures we don't know, given that she never actually skipped class. She started off with stories about museums and exhibitions, but her lies were like an avalanche; they gained velocity and power as they rolled, and not only that, they grew in size too, engulfing everything in their way. At one point she started saying that the teacher was going to take them to visit a madhouse. To which we responded that madhouses didn't exist anymore, and in any case, it seemed unlikely that a primary school teacher would propose that kind of school trip. "I know," she told us confidently, "they're called psychiatric hospitals now. It's a government initiative," she added. "You'll be getting a letter about it soon." I still remember the tone of her voice and the words she picked. Obviously, the letter never arrived, and none of us—neither our parents nor I—ever had the courage to bring it up again, not even as a joke.

SHE DECIDED NOT TO talk anymore and she wrote us the letter you have all seen. It was in January, toward the end of January, I think, though I don't recall the exact date. Now I can say it was only the beginning; it felt like an ending then, but it was only the beginning. I don't know what she finds in silence. Don't ask me; go and find those people who've started following her example. And don't assume I haven't tried to understand her motives. Don't assume we haven't talked about it. Me, my mother, my father: when it first started, her silence gave us a lot to think about. We would contemplate the question for hours: *Why do you think she's doing it? Oh, come on, that can't be it—how can you say that? She's not like that.* Each one of us would come out with some side of her the others didn't know about. At the end of the day, we would separate and take stock of what had emerged, and all of it seemed to make sense. It's funny, isn't it? Whenever we talked about it together, we just didn't get it. But once we were alone, and silent, all the pieces seemed to fall into place. Like those diseases that torture you night and day, but as soon as you're at the doctor's office, the symptoms suddenly disappear. *I've got a rash right in the middle of my back, Doctor, I swear I can't sleep from how itchy it is. What do you mean, you can't see anything? I guess it* has *stopped itching.*

When we were together, we told each other she was doing it as a challenge, to see how long she would last and what effect it would have on her. My father's theory was that she was doing it because she couldn't stand people anymore, which was a trait she had inherited from him. Out of all of us, I think he was the most worried; he could barely sleep from how guilty he felt. His fear was depression. "It runs in the family," he would say. "Your uncle was depressed." And yet he never visited her, not once. He withdrew into some kind of mutism, too, and his life has not been the same since. Whenever they were together, they were like two obsidian walls facing each other, each looking down at their feet, their eyes never meeting.

My mum, on the other hand, was convinced there was a religious or philosophical explanation: she was sure that my sister must be part of a sect, some cult that preached perpetual silence as the elixir of purification. On weekends when we went to see her, she would look for evidence to back up her thesis under the guise of tidying up. In a way, she had predicted what would come to pass.

And what did I believe? At night, when I was alone, I would begin to think that it must have all started with a study of some sort. An exercise. Can we exist without communicating? Would we still be human beings? I would imagine she must have begun like that and followed the path wherever it led her—and the path had led her deeper and deeper into a sinkhole that had neglected to spit her back out. I think, in the end, the silence just reeled her in. I think that's what happened.

She has written us some letters; you've seen them already. She addressed them to me so that I would pass the message on to our parents. She never had the courage to engage with them directly. That's the only thing I blame her for. When you take such a radical step, you have no choice but to take into account how it will reflect on the people around you. On the people who brought you into the world. Ever since the moment you're born, you have certain obligations toward other people. Toward society. It's sad, but that's how it is. I also think that this choice of hers was a desperate attempt to obtain a certain kind of freedom, the same kind that cloistered monks seek through self-deprivation. But you can only obtain freedom for yourself at the expense of other people. It's a selfish choice, like suicide. It's not just your own life; you also have to think about those who are left to face the pain. It's sad, but that's how it is.

SHE COMMUNICATED THROUGH the written word, a written word reduced to its bare bones, as if every word had been rationed. Her messages were less like notes, and then more like stamps on a ration card. Eventually that stopped, too. No more letters, no more messages, nothing of that sort. We went to see her one Saturday, we always went on Saturdays, and she was gone. The last thing she wrote was a note asking us to take care of her fish. The note was stuck to the aquarium with a piece of tape, but the fish wasn't there. We poured out the water, looked in the crevices, among the rocks and the objects she had bought for him, but Harpo had disappeared, just like my sister. Perhaps she'd had a change of heart right at the end and had taken him with her, wherever it was that she'd gone. I like to picture the scene sometimes—it's a funny image. I can see her holding a plastic bag, like a child at the fairground. Or maybe it's a glass bowl that she's holding with both hands, like an astronaut carrying her helmet. "What's that creature?" people ask her. She doesn't reply, so they bend down for a closer look. "That's not a goldfish!" they exclaim, perhaps in horror.

I've read that scorpionfish are edible. So one night I dreamt that she'd eaten him. I woke up with the image of my sister in a dark kitchen, neither her own nor our parents'. Dark and empty, and her standing there with a plate in front of her and her pet fish hanging out of her mouth. I've also read that the species is multiplying in our seas, too. The question is, how did it manage to get here from the Caribbean?

The other possibility is that he simply evaporated. I've always wondered what happened to all the words she never uttered over these past few months. I think some must have sunk to the bottom and turned into pulp, but the majority will have vanished, turned into air—like water, like the soul from a body.

My sister has disappeared and we are left behind, our words setting us apart from her and making us human. It's us, and this army of injudicious strangers who see in her a new redeemer.

THEY TALKED ABOUT her on the news. My mother called me; she was crying, and it was maybe the third time in my life I'd ever heard her cry. "They're talking about your sister," she said. "Have they found her?" I asked, my heart bouncing in my chest. "No," she said. "But they're talking about an article. An article that was published online, about a girl who stopped talking. It's her, it must be her."

I went looking for the article. I found it. It was all anyone on the Internet and social media seemed to be talking about. There was an interview with her. I doubted it was real—my sister would never have agreed. Apart from the letters to us, she hasn't written anything else, I'm sure of it. And she was duty-bound to write those letters; they were a way of proving to us and to herself that she was still human.

Her name is not revealed—not in full, at least. She has taken on the outlines of a prophet, the contours of a legend. But if you think about it, that's very easy to do, these days. Every day, thanks to social media, thanks to the news outlets that subsist on social media, thanks to an endless and unstoppable narration of people's lives, every day we choose somebody to celebrate or denigrate. And that person becomes legend. We don't need to lock ten strangers up in a house anymore; that house has no borders now; that house is our house. She didn't want any of this. She wanted the opposite, but what she got is attention. With no salvation.

THE TRUTH IS, I envied her. There have been moments when I wished I were her. I was five when she was born; she was chubby and adorable, her skin pink and firm like peaches in June. She was passed around from one pair of arms to the next and never made a fuss, and suddenly I had to learn how to get people to notice me, whereas until that moment, it had all been effortless, and I had never needed to ask. I was an awful child and I would take the food out of her mouth when our parents weren't looking, I would tell her, "Fatty, you're a fatty" and hide spoonfuls of her baby food in a napkin instead of feeding it to her. I would steal her toys and throw them in the trash, hiding them under the rest of the rubbish so that my parents wouldn't notice. The only time she cried was when she couldn't find a toy because of me. She'd be inconsolable. So I stopped, because she attracted even more attention that way. The despair that took hold of her when she couldn't find something was more about her sense of order than it was about possessiveness: she has always had a remarkable photographic memory and has always been a creature of habit. It bothered her if some kind of order was disrupted. I have never had the courage to confess to her what I did. She was very little, so she doesn't even remember. I've always been able to count on that, and over the course of the years, I have tried to make it up to her.

I really was a terrible sister. I was jealous. I was jealous of her independence, her certainty, how she went about her existence without seeking other people's approval, as if their acceptance were a burden rather than a source of motivation. I've discovered that new expressions have been invented to describe these feelings: FOMO, which stands for Fear of Missing Out and can sometimes go all the way to social anxiety, and JOMO, the Joy of Missing Out, whose extreme is where I think my sister's condition lies. I have always lived in the shadow of other people, though Cristina always claimed the opposite. I would wake up in the middle of the night from fraught sleep, I would dream that my parents had stopped talking to me, that I had become invisible and they only noticed my presence when I made a mess, moved things around, hid them away. Like a poltergeist. Just like my sister when she was little, I hate a mess. I have always been praised for being a neat and reliable person. People think it's a natural talent; they don't know how much effort there is behind it.

There is nothing natural about preserving a childhood ability. Children are born with a series of qualities that change over time; adults don't accept this. It doesn't matter if the change is negative or positive. If you are precociously intelligent, you'll be the household genius: and when your intelligence reveals its true nature—that is to say, in the majority of cases, as an inherited quality that you have not received in greater measure but merely a little earlier than everyone else—and falls back in line with that of other kids your age, your parents will perceive this as the ultimate defeat. Conversely, an irritating character trait—like pettiness, prickliness, or grouchiness—will remain in place even after you've created a sense of personal identity, even after you've reconstructed a sense of personal identity, and no matter how hard you might have tried to improve yourself.

I was the balanced and agreeable child, and it's taken me a whole lifetime to hold on to that qualification. I was also the less observed child; being reliable implies a certain degree of freedom. One time I missed my curfew by an hour, just to see if they'd notice. They did notice, but they blamed my sister. It was around the time they'd started asking me to take her with me when I went out, since she didn't have many friends.

Last week I went to the dentist. He was chatting to the dental hygienist while they gave me a filling. They were talking a bunch of nonsense about mortgage interest rates, and I knew they were wrong but I couldn't show them why. I wanted to say my piece but my mouth was being held wide open by a cheek retractor and was being occupied by all their tools, so I was scared to even whimper—lest the movement of a muscle, however infinitesimally small, might jolt the instrument vibrating in my mouth and send it right into areas where there was no anesthesia, such as my palate or my upper lip, scarring me for life or causing me pain. I couldn't respond to them, so I decided to wait until they were done, gripping the arms of the chair.

At a certain point the hygienist noticed what I was doing and said: "Are we hurting you?" The dentist stopped and I whimpered and shook my head, no, no, and I let them get on with their work, even though the urge to speak was making my chest and my limbs tingle. The filling took a few more minutes to complete, and when I was finally in a position to speak, the tingling was gone. The hygienist and the doctor had moved on to a different subject, and it did not make sense anymore to point out that they had been talking rubbish. The moment had passed.

It occurred to me that if I had done something sooner, if I had spoken out, I would have ended up coming across as rude, despite my best intentions. I always try not to do that. I have been teaching my son not to impose himself on other people; I tell him that there are many different ways of thinking and there's no guarantee yours is the right one. But recently there has been so much drivel being peddled as truth that it is becoming harder and harder to keep quiet. Still, in that particular moment, I understood. It was as if time—that brief fragment of time during which the dentist had removed the decay in my tooth and replaced it with fresh material—had cleansed me, and that tingling I'd felt had been nothing but a flash of fever, a momentary rise in body temperature designed to flush out the virus of intolerance and rage. The things that had been said, just like the things I would have wanted to say, no longer mattered. And so I thought of Cristina. I understood what she meant when she talked about purification.

I NEEDED TO talk to someone who knew her. I mean knew her in a different way. That's why I got in touch with Silvia. Silvia had gotten into the habit of coming to our house back when she was in high school; my sister was a rather insecure teenager, and insecure teenagers commonly attach themselves to histrionic and centralizing personalities like Silvia. Silvia's family life was problematic, and she was always pleased to spend time away from home. I think her father was violent, perhaps only verbally, but unsurprisingly, she did not like to talk about it, and my sister—well, she's always been the best person to confess a secret to. My mother never liked Silvia, but I think she was just jealous of her relationship with Cristina and worried about my sister's grades, which had suffered once they had started spending time together. On the other hand, my sister had also started going out more. To me this was liberating, and I was grateful to Silvia for it. It isn't good for a teenager not to have friends.

Silvia was often inappropriate, but I have always appreciated her slightly rough personality—not exactly rude, but not particularly refined either. She's one of those people who are incapable of adjusting their manner and tone to the context they're in, either because they lack that kind of intelligence or because they're so bold as to not give a damn—and I think this quirk of hers in particular may have caused her to rise in Cristina's estimation. They grew apart during their university years, when Silvia got it into her head that she was going to become a model. I couldn't really imagine someone like her in a such a manufactured environment, and I was saddened when it initially seemed to work, because that wild, impetuous side to Silvia is so far from my own personality, and so rarely found in people, and it always upsets me to see the world tear it to pieces and turn it into indifference and arrogance. But when Silvia came back to Turin and they rekindled their friendship, I began to realize that she hadn't changed too much. Maybe she was a little more disillusioned, a veil clouding her gaze every now and then, an awareness that finished her sentences for her, all of which made me like her even more.

I had Silvia's number saved back from their high school days, and I texted her to ask if we could meet up. She replied to me the next day, after I'd already given up on her—though I pictured her as the kind of person who left her phone lying around or forgot that she had received a message she should probably reply to. She told me she was free that afternoon and suggested we meet for a coffee, sending me a location for a bar that was quite far from the city center, where I knew she'd bought an apartment. I told her I finished work at five and would meet her there. I asked my mother to look after Elia, using a made-up doctor's appointment as my excuse.

I was late, but Silvia got there even later. When she arrived, I was already sitting at a table. I saw very clearly how the whole bar turned to look at her. She was wearing a pair of baggy jeans, red ankle boots, and a leather jacket: nothing particularly striking, but her long, tousled hair made her look like Liv Tyler in the video for *Crazy*. She smiled at me and apologized for being late, making some excuse. As she talked, I wondered if she had figured out why I had contacted her.

"What will you have?" she says. "This bar makes great cocktails. Have you eaten already or do you want food?"

I was still curious as to why she had suggested meeting here, so far from everything, but I couldn't find a moment to ask. Silvia talked nonstop, and when she wasn't talking, she looked around or fixed her gaze on me to make sure I ordered something, like a mother with her malnourished daughter. I did not recall her having been so solicitous. In fact, the most amusing thing about Silvia (and the one thing I was willing to bet my sister envied most about her) was her inability to worry more about others than she did about herself. Which, for a person as anxious as me, or as introverted as Cristina, was incredibly relaxing. But Silvia didn't do this in the irritating manner of an egocentric; she reminded me more of the pure and carefree way children act. Yet that day, for the first time ever, she was making me agitated. The only explanation I could think of was that she must feel guilty.

"Actually, I don't think I want a cocktail—I'll have a glass of red instead. Get them to make a suggestion, they're good. Shall we also get the charcuterie board?"

"I'll have some wine, too," I tell her. I realize these are the first words I've spoken since we got there, greetings aside. I feel like it's been an eternity. "Agreed on the charcuterie board. I'm hungry."

Silvia turns toward the counter and motions at the barman, who comes round to serve us personally. There's only a few other people there, and from the way they address each other, I gather that Silvia must be a regular. The barman brings us two glasses of nebbiolo and a tray of cold cuts and canapés, and Silvia begins to relax.

"So, how's it going?" I ask her. "Are you working at the moment?"

"On and off," she says, her mouth full of canapé. "I've gone back to university. Preparing for when I'm older and no one wants me anymore, you know. Like right now. I'm in that phase where no one even considers you. Too young for hearing-aid commercials or adult diapers, and too late to shake my ass in front of the camera. It's not as firm as it used to be. My ass, I mean. Not the camera."

"Aren't they looking for better representation, these days?"

"Not if you're in your thirties. What they want is extremes. A small part that can stand in for the whole. Thirty is the bland midpoint when no one gives a shit about you. What do you represent, when you're thirty? You're not young, you're not old, you're not middle-aged."

"What are you studying?"

"Psychology. Like all girls with daddy issues."

It's not difficult to be silent when you're with Silvia. The people she interacts with are spectators, content to stick to their roles. Just like sitting in front of the TV in the evening. Her phone is on the table, I can see the screen constantly lighting up, but it's on silent. I guess they must be Instagram notifications. I have Instagram but I don't use it much. I'd stopped following Silvia because she bored me. Particularly since they'd introduced stories to the platform, and in order to match what her colleagues were doing, she had begun posting them too, almost daily, from her bed or while she was walking down the street. It all seemed so silly to me. In those moments, I struggled to recognize her. It wasn't really her. I wondered if my sister had had the same feeling, before she'd signed off social media altogether.

"What have you been up to?"

She asks me about Cristina before I have a chance to bring her up. "It's her, isn't it?" she adds, lowering her voice. I ask her what she's referring to. "The girl they're talking about. The one who started this whole idiotic trend." I tell her that I haven't heard from Cristina in months and I was hoping she might have some news for me.

"What do you mean, you haven't heard from her? I haven't seen her since March. Or April."

I tell her I wasn't aware of that.

"Of course not. How could you be? We didn't fall out, no. I'm the one who stepped away. I still feel guilty about it. I love her, but what she's doing is lethal. How do you guys cope with it? I tried. Are you sure she's all right?"

I tell her about the letters we receive every week, bang on time. Our Monday morning post.

"What does she say?"

"Nothing. Just a white piece of paper inside a white envelope. All it says on the piece of paper is a number, written in red felt-tip pen: 1, 2, 3, 4, and so on, in sequence. A new number every week."

"How do you know it's her?"

"Who else could it be? It's her handwriting."

"And I guess you can't trace the sender."

"No. That would require a full investigation."

"Have you reported it to the police?"

"We tried. But they say there's nothing to follow up on, given that she's disappeared by choice and provided an explanation. If you could even call it an explanation. And the fact that we are getting news of her in some way suggests that she is fine."

"Why numbers?"

"She's always loved numbers, remember? She used to say they're alive and dead at the same time. Concrete and abstract. They don't communicate any emotions. Something like that."

Silvia shakes her head. "You see?" she says. "That's the whole point. I told her a thousand times. Not communicating is impossible. It's not animal behavior, it's superhuman. And she's not superhuman. No matter how much she tells herself otherwise. She is still communicating in some way."

I consider her point. She is right. Cristina is worried about us.

"What do your parents think?" she asks.

"Never mind that," I say. "Listen. Do you really not know where she is? You really have no idea?"

Silvia takes a sip of wine, then says: "I'm the last person she would have told." She takes out some tobacco from her handbag and starts rolling a cigarette. "Want to step outside with me?"

It has begun to rain in light, irritating, early autumn drops. We take cover under the balcony of the floor above. "Could I have one?" I ask her. I haven't smoked in years. My fingernails are a disaster. Silvia has the most beautiful hands I have ever seen. Semipermanent pastel pink nail polish, on almond-shaped nails.

"I stopped contacting her in April. Toward the end, I used to come home after going to see her and find that I couldn't sleep. I would have to sit there with the lights and the TV on, my phone at hand. With the shutters and the windows closed, I would convince myself that someone could just walk past in the middle of the night and wake me up as soon as I managed to fall asleep. And I live on the top floor, you know. The point is, all that silence got inside of me somehow and came back out precisely when I was alone, sitting beside me like a ghost. I've always thought her choice was bullshit, the most selfish thing a person could do. But I believed I could tolerate it. It irritated me, it infuriated me, but I could tolerate it. After all, it's what people like me dream about, right? Egocentrics like me. Someone who will sit quietly and listen to them. I had a cat when I was little, a Ragdoll," she says, pausing to take a drag.

I'm amazed at Silvia's ability to talk so quickly while also smoking. I'd be coughing my lungs out.

"You know, the really expensive, really hairy ones with empty blue eyes. A gift from my parents, to keep me company. He fulfilled his role perfectly: I would talk to him for hours and he would sit there, motionless, with those baby-doll eyes fixed on me. When I came home from school in the afternoons it was me and him, and I would confess to him the things I didn't have the courage to tell anyone else. One day I came home and he wasn't there. My father had left a window open and the cat had run away. My brother teased me, said that I'd stupefied the cat with my endless talking, but I didn't really believe him. I cried for days, and the cat never came back. So I began to think that all of my words, all the things I had confessed to him, were still in there, somewhere inside of him, and now they were free and roaming the world, and I could stop worrying about it all. They wouldn't torture me anymore. It's a stupid story, I know, but I've been thinking about it a lot, recently. That's not how it went with Cristina. She wanted to be like an animal, or like a rock, but it's impossible. It's not like talking to a cat that stares at you and can't reply, it's not like screaming at the heavens or at a mountain. Cristina's silence has a motive and a purpose—that's what I've been saying since the beginning. You can't do something like that just for yourself. We are human beings, and that's one of the many luxuries we can't afford."

"So why do you think she did it?" I ask her.

"At first she approached it as an exercise, a test. Then it became a vice. If I were to venture into some armchair psychoanalysis—the only kind I can do, for the time being—I'd tell you that more than anything else, what lies behind it is fear."

"Of what?"

"Of pain, obviously. If you're not human—if you're a chair, or a tree, or a stone—you can't feel pain, right? Other people's thoughts, their judgments, they no longer exist; people don't trouble you, they don't worry you—it's just you and what you observe."

"So you don't think it was exhaustion, then. That she hated people so much that she wanted to be rid of them."

Silvia lets the smoke out with a little laugh. "I'm not a particularly clever person. And I was terrible at high school, as you know. But I remember that in one of the handful of philosophy classes I actually was there for, not smoking outside, and more or less paying attention, they mentioned a philosopher who talked about suicide. Kant? Schopenhauer?"

"Both, I think."

"I think it was Schopenhauer. Cristina would know."

"Aren't you supposed to take philosophy classes during first-year psychology?"

"That's in the second semester. Anyway, he was basically saying that people who commit suicide don't hate life; they love it so much that it disappoints them. And suicide is no more than a manifestation of extreme love. Something like that."

"Yes, I think I remember that."

"Well, I think—and always have thought—that withdrawing

from a person is the purest way of declaring your love for them. It's the same with words. I don't think it's ever been a cry for help. That's not what she was missing. But just as suicide reaffirms life, so silence reaffirms words. That's good, isn't it? I'm going to save it for my exam."

She inhales a mouthful of smoke, her nearly finished cigarette disappearing between her sharp-tipped nails. They look like the hands of a doll; she could be cutting throats with those nails. They scare me and attract me at the same time.

"I was worried too, at first. Then I thought it best to let her be. It sounds like a contradiction—and it may seem a little cowardly, too—but eventually I too began to believe that this purification process would benefit her. Like when you cry and then feel better afterward. Like children when they misbehave. Does your son do that?"

"All the time."

"So do my nephews. My brother stops paying attention to them and they immediately start squeezing out tears, snot, and sobs—they're like a blocked toilet. Once the moment has passed, they're the ones who come looking for you again, and suddenly they're the world's most docile kids. Even their faces look different. As if anger were a demon that needs kicking out, a spot to squeeze. Excuse my imagery. Shall we go back inside?"

"People on social media say that children misbehave because they don't know how to communicate their discomfort. That they just want to be heard but haven't learned an effective way to ask for that."

"Cristina would say that social media is full of shit. Sometimes I agree with her."

We go back into the bar; there are some cold cuts left on the board. I finish the wine in my glass while Silvia orders another.

I do the same, to keep her company, even though I have to drive afterward. We talk about trivial things. Neither of us is hungry anymore.

"Where do you think she went?" Silvia asks at one point.

"I have a different answer every day," I reply. "Recently I've convinced myself that she must be somewhere crowded. Somewhere far away from here."

I DON'T TELL her about my dream. Sometimes I wake up in the middle of the night feeling relieved, and sure that Cristina has returned. But the further sleep retreats, the more the feeling fades. So all I can do is think back to the dream I've just had, concentrating on the details, clinging to them as a means of retracing my way through the tunnel. I often dream that she is in Asia, in a giant metropolis, hiding among the many thousands of faces you see there in a day, on the streets or on the subway. Sometimes, I think of Japan. I have never been there, but I saw a documentary on TV a few months ago. People rigorously queuing up, and every ritual elevated so as to communicate as little about the self as possible. The silence on public transport. People switching their phones off or turning the sound down before getting on the metro, where phone calls are forbidden. Temples and Zen, that devout order which harks to some superior, impalpable reality, the cold, freezing sense of peace that derives from observing wood, basalt, sand, with no interruptions, as if in a state of hypnosis. The tidy queues, nobody trying to push through. In order to make all this absence bearable, there are places dedicated to noise, to entertainment, secluded places where you can let go and let it out. Elsewhere, silence. *Ishin-denshin*, said the documentary: what the mind thinks, the heart transmits. Teaching without words, from the disciple to the pupil. From heart to heart, from mind to mind. Cristina would thrive in a place like that.

Sometimes, before I fall asleep, I picture her in the airport, in one of those airless chapels where people go to pray for their flight to land safely, or to meditate, or to sit down if there's nowhere else available. Other times I see her on a rapid and soundless train, one that makes only an imperceptible rustle, like a bird of prey or leaves in the wind, my sister with her head turned toward the window, looking out at landscapes I have not seen, thinking things I cannot know.

Silvia gives me a guy's phone number. His name is Daniele; he dated my sister for a while. She suggests I contact him. She confesses she's already talked to him herself. He doesn't know where Cristina is either; they stopped seeing each other months ago. But he might be useful in some way.

I send him a message; he replies a few hours later. We arrange to meet the following Sunday. I suggest Valentino Park, and it turns out to be a lovely autumn day. Autumn was—is—Cristina's favorite season. Daniele is kind; he says he regrets that he can't really help me.

"I haven't seen her in six months. She decided she didn't want to see me anymore. How did it all blow up like this? Everyone's talking about her. The other day my mother told me that our neighbor has stopped speaking. It's like a nightmare."

"My uncle has also taken it up," I tell him. "Cristina would say it's like killing in the name of God. Unconstitutional."

"Yes, I remember she used to say things like that," he says.

When he feels safe, he shows me a letter. It's got my sister's signature, and it's dated September 3. Five days before she disappeared.

It isn't much help. Aside from a series of private confessions regarding her feelings for this guy, it says only things I already knew.

Before we part ways, Daniele tells me in a whisper: "I've got Harpo. I found him on the landing outside my door one day. Inside a plastic box, like the kind you store food in. I'm looking after him."

I tell him that if he'd like, he can come and get the fish tank. I have the keys to Cristina's apartment.

I REMEMBER A family lunch from months ago, after she'd already stopped talking. My mother had invited our uncle, whom we had always liked until he started believing in conspiracy theories and getting involved with far-right ideologies. But at the end of the day, he's still her brother, as my mother reminds us during every holiday season, and insufferable as she finds him, her overriding feeling toward him is of pity. He is a very lonely man; he spends more time on his computer than he does in the world. He even consorts with flat-earthers. In any event, my mother feels guilty if he spends holidays on his own, so he appears at our house every now and then.

During Easter lunch, he came out with yet another surreal theory of his, something to do with reptilians, this idea that the DNA of the earth's most powerful people has been spliced with that of extraterrestrial lizards. I stopped trying to argue against his claims a long time ago, because I know there's no point. I can see that he has found a raison d'être in these opinions he holds, in this feeling that he belongs to a separate self-sustaining class of humans who need no external encouragement, and who are constantly telling one another that they are different from everyone else, more intelligent and more aware than all the other people, who follow social norms like sheep. I have no qualms about letting him think all that. Cristina, on the other hand, has always struggled to bite her tongue. Yet at Easter she just sat there in her corner, her mouth busy nibbling on breadsticks, one hand wringing the napkin on her lap. Or maybe I only paid attention to these details because I was the one secretly raging. To tell the truth, she seemed pretty calm. Maybe the purification had already begun to take effect. It was as if the impetuous side of her, the part that was least capable of adapting to certain situations, had been shut away in a cupboard. Like an expensive dress you've worn in the past, but every time you've put it on, something's gone wrong, so you've become convinced that the dress is to blame, and since it reminds you of negative thoughts, you've let it get buried behind other clothes.

The fact is that my sister hates hypocrisy. The lie forcefully told, not defending but defining, uttered without any question to prompt it. Lies, she would say, are like sunglasses: they're not there to alter your vision, but to protect your eyesight from the rays of the sun. It's as if she had never stepped over that threshold of purity that children are granted, as if she had never developed the requisite antibodies. I still remember the day she discovered that Santa Claus isn't real. She was eight or nine years old and came home crying. My mother asked her what had happened. She told us that one of her classmates had asked the teacher if it was true that Santa was an adult invention, as his parents had decided to tell him. He had put his hand up and asked this question in front of the whole class. The teacher could have changed the subject, could have stalled, could have said anything at all, but what she told them was: It's true. Your parents are Santa Claus. They're the ones buying the presents, eating the cookies, drinking the glass of milk, putting your presents under the tree. There is no reindeer sleigh. No big-bellied old man with a white beard who delivers presents to every child in the world over the course of a single night. You're not so little anymore. It's only right that you should know.

At least that is what Cristina told us. Soon all the parents were up in arms and, in their fury, went en masse to speak to the teacher. She tried to justify her actions by saying that she had been caught by surprise and would have never said a word if one of the children hadn't brought it up. But she had always thought this to be a deplorable tradition, a socially sanctioned lie. It was about time we stopped.

That day my sister discovered, in the most abrupt possible way, that parents lie. That adults lie. Now that I think about it, maybe that's how her own lying phase began. My sister's rebellion started the day she decided to mete out to the world—to adults—the same treatment she had been subjected to. Isn't that how it always goes? The loss of innocence, I mean. Doesn't it start the day we discover that Santa Claus isn't real?

MY FATHER LOVES RIDDLES. He's never been a particularly affectionate father, you know. He has always loved us deeply, but he is one of those people in whom affection manifests itself as a series of behaviors designed to cause as little disruption as possible. To limit disruption. He took us to school every day to spare us the school bus, or he'd pick us up when he wasn't working. He was cautious when he told us off. He has always been meek: my grandmother used to say about him that "wherever you leave him, he'll stay put." She claimed the same was true of me. She was much more similar to my mother and to Cristina, and I never understood whether she meant it as a compliment or an insult.

In any event, my father always showed us affection, but in that slightly detached, absent way that only fathers can manage (in the best-case scenario). The kind of father who could never say no to us. Or who would tell you, when you sought his permission to go out at night, to "go and ask your mother." Not a huge amount of effort, but he was always there. Anyway, as I was saying, when you peel away his outer layer of normality, he too has his own peculiarities, one of which is his passion for riddles. One of his favorites, when we were little, was: *If you say my name, I disappear. Who am I?* My father loved watching us squirm. He refused to tell us the answer to his puzzles until one of us guessed it, not even if we begged him to, but he did give us as much time as we needed. We were allowed to come up with theories, and we could have as many guesses as we liked; we could ask him questions, provided they could be answered with a yes or a no. The only thing we could not do was ask for outside help: we couldn't involve Mum, or our grandparents, or other people. We had to come up with the solution ourselves.

My sister and I would run around the house in circles, picking up pen and paper, drawing diagrams, writing down the possibilities. I had the advantage of being older, and at first Cristina would give up very quickly. But as she grew up, it became less of a team game and more of a personal battle. *If you say my name, I disappear.* Do you know the answer? If you think about it, it's easy enough. I was the one who guessed the answer, that time. Cristina was eight years old and came up with a series of wrong answers, all of which were far too concrete. Back then, silence had not yet entered her field of vision. Until she decided to make it real. A material act in response to an emotional state that was, even to us, impossible to comprehend.

I HAVE NEVER stopped to think about how social media may have affected our relationship. I'll do that now, for the first time. I remember very well when my father installed the Internet at home. We'd had a desktop computer for a few years already, situated in my mother's study. She had started using one for her work at the school, to type out exercises or coursework assignments and also print them out. Whenever she didn't need it, my father would use it to play games. His colleagues had given him copies of certain video games: *Tomb Raider*, *Monkey Island*, *Super Mario*, *Prince of Persia*. He would go into the study after dinner and pick up wherever he'd left off. Sometimes he played before dinner too, and my mother—immensely disappointed by this behavior—would have to call him at least three times before he came and joined us at the table. I was around eleven or twelve back then, and occasionally I would agree to try and play myself, while he sat there giving me advice and teaching me all the tricks, though I was never very good.

Cristina was younger, and although some of the games were still too difficult for her, she loved sitting on my father's lap and watching him play. They were louder than usual during those moments: they encouraged each other, yelling gleefully every time they reached another checkpoint and lamenting every defeat. My mother and I would take it as an opportunity for us to spend some time alone together; if I didn't have homework to do, I would help her out in the kitchen or set the table, and in the meantime, we would talk. Now that I think about it, there has always been a small kind of family rift based on words: my mother and I were the talkative ones and kept no secrets from each other, while my sister and my father were brought together by a different kind of sharing, a silent one, more practical than language-based.

The Internet arrived in our home in the year 2000, and at the time it did not cause much of a change. My father and Cristina continued to play video games and make the occasional foray online, though these incursions were rare and brief, given that the cost of the Internet at the time was determined by how much you used it. I was now fourteen, and whenever the computer was not being used for video games, I was allowed to seek out photographs and information on my favorite actors and singers, though always under my parents' supervision. There was also the occasional argument between my mother and my father when she picked up the phone in the middle of one of my father's online gaming sessions to call a friend or our grandmother, forgetting every time that the 56K modem was connected to the telephone line.

Soon we moved on to ADSL. Having an email address became useful at first, then indispensable; we started hearing about social media, initially at a remove until eventually, without even realizing when this had happened, we were all on it, our parents even more in the thick of things than we were. This is where my mother unexpectedly outstripped us all: at last her yearning for a network, for communication, had an easy outlet, well within reach. All of a sudden, Cristina and I found our newsfeeds teeming with kittens, recipes, local news; and when we got together for lunch or dinner on Sundays, my mother would pick up her phone right after dessert or sit at the computer—which had by now migrated to the living room—and scroll endlessly and without restraint through the Facebook home page. "I found the girl I used to share a desk with at school," she'd say. "I hadn't heard from her in years. She's moved to the Canary

Islands. To the Canary Islands, can you believe it? I should go and visit her." These were the positive effects for someone like her, who had always felt it was rude to end any relationship in the absence of a genuine slight.

But there were negatives, too. "Did you see what they're saying? Vaccines are bad for you." "There's so much violence around these days, it's starting to scare me." "Do you really think they haven't found a cure for cancer yet? Impossible. They have one and they're saving it for the rich." But there was a way to counter this. We took it upon ourselves to debunk every false claim she relayed to us, bringing evidence to support our position, pointing out that rich people die too, showing her studies and data. Cristina was always very active in these battles; she's the kind of person who loves having the last word. Loved, I should say. Anyway, it worked.

My mother has always been a reasonable person. But what we couldn't stop was her constant sharing. Every day there were ten new items on her home page—video recipes, events, photos of my son. Instead of making videos of your grandson so you can post them online, why don't you just spend time with him *in real life*? But in her mind, there was no distinction. "Your sister's gone off Facebook," she told me in September last year. I hadn't even noticed. "Do you think there's something wrong?" I told her that social media was not a litmus test for happiness, and if a person looks happy on Facebook, it doesn't necessarily mean they are. "I'm perfectly aware of that, thank you," she replied. "I may be old, but I'm not stupid." She was right. She had noticed something the rest of us had missed. If we had listened to my mother, maybe we could have helped my sister. If only I had interpreted that act as a prodrome, as the first symptom of a degenerative disease, maybe my sister wouldn't have gotten to this point. But she has always loved having the last word, and the last word is silence.

WHAT ARE MY parents saying now? My father's lost at least five kilograms, maybe ten. We don't know the exact figure because if he weighs himself, he does so in secret, and he refuses to go to the doctor. He isn't eating much, and what little he does eat he seems to swallow with great reluctance. When we visit my parents, we bring warmth and sounds, and sometimes even laughter, especially when my son—who does not take after his aunt but is still learning how to manage the urge to communicate—gets his words all mixed up. My father smiles, he tries to, but the toll it's taking on him is clear to see. It's obvious from the way he removes himself from the conversation, the way he stares into space or focuses his gaze on some detail—his own hands, say, or a fly on the tablecloth—forgetting everything else.

On my mother, the pain—though perhaps I should say concern; I don't like to use the word *pain*, as if it were all over already, as if there were no hope—is less evident. But she's simply better at dissimulating. My mother has never been particularly pious, but she has that positivity that can usually be found in religious people. She is so optimistic that at times she can come across as detached, selfish, and lacking emotion. She is capable of throwing epic tantrums when she does not get what she wants—an object or a grocery item she had planned to buy but cannot be found, a lack of availability on the day she'd hoped to go to the salon, a recipe that hasn't turned out perfectly—while remaining impassive when faced with the suffering of others. "I'm not impassive, I'm pragmatic. Optimistic," she might say, responding to defeat and disappointment with proposed solutions, in an attempt to leave no stone unturned.

If there's anyone Cristina resembles, in her lack of empathy around the kind of decision she has taken, that would certainly be my mother. Indeed, my mother's blunt approach is not limited to the suffering of others; she treats herself the same way, too. If we were to try and identify the deeper motivations behind this, as I have tried to do a thousand times rather than resign myself to the fact that I have a selfish mother, we could interpret her attitude as a protective stance, maternal instinct in its purest form. The mother rabbit who spends time away from her kittens so as to avoid drawing a predator's attention to their nest. The problem with this approach is that it can be exhausting, especially in those moments when all you really need is a shoulder to cry on—a silent shoulder, someone who will listen to you and sympathize with you. Perhaps one of the many unexpected side effects of my sister's silence is that it has transformed her into something she has never been: understanding, delicate, yielding.

THE FACT IS, she never wanted any of this. Her silence was personal, not a universal battle. Then people decided to emulate her, and so she disappeared. I'm beginning to think that the problem with humanity is that stupid people are full of words, while intelligent people are full of doubt. So this is all useless, because anyone who has anything to say will think it unimportant and keep quiet instead. The winners will be people who talk about themselves and feel they are better than other people. This wave of silence is not a very effective vaccine. She did not want any of this. She wanted to do it for herself. When did that become a luxury we can no longer afford? If we are stripped of the chance to assert our selfishness, what's left for us?

She wrote me many letters, but I never understood. Only now am I beginning to do so. I'd like to tell her: *You're right.*

The condition of being human comes, first and foremost, with a series of duties. One of these is the duty to communicate. There's no escape from it, there's no reprieve, unless you isolate yourself from other people. And even that is sending a message.

Have you noticed how everything eventually becomes a trend? My grandmother would tell me that every time she gave me any of her old clothes. I didn't like them: they were too big for me, they had shoulder pads, the skirts were too long, the colors too muted. "People will laugh at me if I wear these, Grandma. No one dresses like this now," I'd tell her. She would say: "They'll be back in fashion in a few years' time, you'll see." I'd take them anyway, just to make her happy, because she hated it when things were thrown away or abandoned. She considered objects to be like people. Afterward, with my mother's consent, we would donate everything to charity shops. But maybe my grandmother was right: everything eventually lands, or returns, in a display window. And right now, in the wake of all that hypercommunication, at a time when even the most complex, the most fundamental battles can seemingly be fought just by posting about your intention to do so, as if simply intending to do something somehow made us the people we are—right now, as I was saying, silence is what's fashionable. And now, having thus been observed, codified, proclaimed, imposed, and avenged, it has disappeared, just like in my father's riddle.

They've killed silence. They've proven her right. It doesn't mean anything anymore.

How will this whole thing end? I have no idea. I can't predict the future. It might keep growing or it might fizzle out, a passing trend like so many others, a few hashtags and that's it, for things always look bigger on the Internet than they actually are. Right now, social networks are seeing an unprecedented drop in sign-ups and record numbers of people deactivating their accounts, anywhere between fifty and seventy percent of users, according to some estimates, but we do not have the precise data, as the platforms won't disclose it. The newspapers write, "The party of silence has won," and countless words are being committed to paper to describe or attempt to comprehend this phenomenon, but nobody knows its true size. It could grow beyond measure or end quite soon; there are different schools of thought on this.

I can't form any opinion on the matter; I've never been particularly good at deciphering the present. Now that I think about it, that's what my sister used to say about herself. But she has always had strong analytical capabilities and a critical sensibility; she loved forming an opinion on something and expressing it, if the circumstances were conducive to it. Once her lying phase was over, the truth became, for my sister, an expression of trust, and at times also of affection—to be bestowed on certain people only. Voicing her opinion was no longer a way to gain acceptance, but to test a person or a particular relationship. Now her silence is democratic and all-embracing; there is no hierarchy to it anymore. It does not reflect proximity; nor does it signal any kind of belonging. "In the Beginning Was the Silence," read the headlines in some other newspapers. *The silent generation. The silent revolution*, like in that German film where a group of secondary school kids decide to observe a minute of silence to commemorate the victims of the Hungarian revolt of 1956 and end up being persecuted by the Stasi for it.

Except that in this case, the minutes are infinite and the motivation is, in each case, personal and general. *The silent period:* a stage in language acquisition during which there is a nearly total absence of speech in favor of a focus on listening, elaboration, and the attribution of meanings to words. In their desperate attempts to find some way of describing this absence, some journalists have borrowed or improperly deployed this term despite not understanding its meaning. I'm keeping a copy of every article I can get my hands on, just like my father used to do when we were little and we were mentioned in the local-interest section of the daily *La Stampa* for some school project we had worked on or some minor sporting triumph. Today my sister is revered by a whole army of silent warriors who are willing to sacrifice their words in honor of some nameless god—a god like any other, inaccessible and uninterested, a god that does not manifest itself, that provides no healing, but has the power to make them feel unified: all of them the same, all of them different, all of them magnificently special, important, irreplaceable, and loved.

Elevation

I'VE FOUND HER. Don't ask me to tell you where, because I won't. It doesn't even matter anymore; the movement has taken a shape of its own, separating from her like a cancerous cell from its healthy mother. But I will not tell you where she is. I've already said too much.

I know where she is and I see her every day. I go there and I wash her, because although she's awake, she does not move. I think she's always awake, actually, and I think she never sleeps; her eyes are wide open and her skin is shriveled, so I wash her and slather her with moisturizer and two layers of lip balm, as she uses her lips only to eat and to drink and they look like butterfly wings—I touch them softly so that they won't break. She looks at me for a moment, then gazes into nothing. What do I read into those few seconds of contact? Gratitude. Followed by emptiness. But it's not an abyss; there's no vertigo at the edge of that void. I'm no longer worried about her. I've found her and she's safe. The emptiness takes the shape of my body, like a warm bed, untouched, the mattress cradling your back after a really bad day.

I feed her and she lets me. She prefers semi-liquid foods, like velouté and ice cream. Food that needs chewing bothers her. I can see it in her eyes, in the way she tilts her head. She considers her mouth to be an infected organ, a source of regret, something to apologize for, like inflamed bronchi spewing out phlegm into a crowd of strangers sitting in a waiting room. It's a sensitive membrane that needs protecting. It's a source of shame.

Liquid foods are easier; they fulfill their duty with discretion and leave no trace. I make do by blending everything, from fruit to carbohydrates. I try to put in as many calories as possible, and I know my mother would be proud of me. Cristina is very thin, very weak, as if all the words she did not speak over these past few months had remained inside her, infecting her, consuming the nutrients meant for her, a tapeworm, a parasite. Maybe that's what speech, gestures, writing are for: to ensure that we are not poisoned by the thoughts we have not set free.

But some days I see things differently. Her body does not seem thin anymore, only small. When I arrive in the morning and find her swaddled in blankets, she looks to me like an egg that is incubating itself. I stay by her side, I take care of her, I make sure to be gentle so as not to damage her. Fish die if you touch them; butterflies stop flying. Human beings are alien creatures, venomous, and contact with us can cause the wilting of certain types of pure and rarefied beauty.

I've found her, but I won't tell you where she is. I already regret having said this much. There are no words that can describe what it is for the divine to make itself manifest before our eyes. That moment when you finish a book or a movie you've enjoyed and preserve that sensation that makes your chest expand, keeping it to yourself. And you already know, deep down, that nothing you could say could possibly compare to the grace your body experienced in that moment.

My sister's favorite word—before she refused them all—was *ineffable*.

And as the world outside seems to suddenly go quiet, no more sirens or car engines or dogs barking at the moon, I hear a sound from the bedroom. Maybe it's just my imagination—I'm not that sure. It's not exactly a voice, more of a lament. A lament that strives to be a voice. It does not seem to come from an adult, but neither is it the sound of an animal. It's more of a gurgling from the cradle, a newborn's lallation. *Lallation*—is that the word? It's such a weird word to say out loud. *Lallation*, yes. It's an onomatopoeia. It tastes of milk and a soft palate. My sister's voice from the other room has the delicate, clumsy timbre of a baby's. No fully formed words, only sounds and syllables. I barely breathe, limiting my movements for fear of spoiling it all. I tiptoe closer to where she is and sit on the floor. It sounds like a new language, as fresh as newly fallen snow. Like when we were little girls and, the morning after a snowy night, we would race each other out of the house to see who could leave her footprints on the courtyard first. Sitting on the floor at the threshold, I give myself permission to stay for as long as needed, and to listen, while outside, the garbage trucks begin their rounds.

Acknowledgments

After many years of strenuous research and a painful drafting process, it is only thanks to certain people's support that this book has reached its finished form.

Thanks to everyone at La Nave di Teseo, and particularly Elisabetta Sgarbi, for their immediate and ongoing faith in me. Thanks to Chiara Spaziani, editor and friend, for the attention and the freedom she has gifted to this novel.

Thanks to Anna Haddelsey, Kristi Murray, and the Wylie Agency for their support. Thanks to Ekin Oklap for being, among other things, my first reader, and for alleviating doubt and discouragement with wisdom and empathy.

Thanks to Isabella Borghese for her ready cooperation. Thanks to Daniela Guglielmino for her suggestions and her appreciation. Thanks to Marco Amerighi, Alessandra Minervini, and Carmelo Vetrano for their encouragement and their friendship. Thanks to Dr. Cristina Di Nardo, and to the many conversations, books, films, social media profiles, podcasts, blogs, and articles that both preceded and accompanied the writing of this book, in particular Susan Sontag's essay "The Aesthetics of Silence" and Remo Bassetti's *Storia e Pratica del Silenzio* ("The History and Practice of Silence").

Thanks to Giulia Muscatelli for being a constant source of help and inspiration, for having saved Cristina so many times, for that dinner at the end of March—which, as we would later discover, turned out to be memorable for a variety of reasons—and for teaching me care and tenderness, which have filled (not just) this book with light.

Thanks to my friends, to my sprawling, chaotic, and loving family, to Anna and Filippo Manfredi, Michele Prencipe, Federica Fugazzotto, and Marino Rama for their advice and their suggestions. Thanks to the places that are familiar to me and to the people who inhabit them, even those who are no longer with us; thanks to my mother, trusted reader and adviser, and to my father, for their support, their love, and for having passed on to me a passion for stories.

Thanks to Enrico for drawing me away from silence, for showing me patience, purity, and, most of all, the beauty of truthful and essential words.